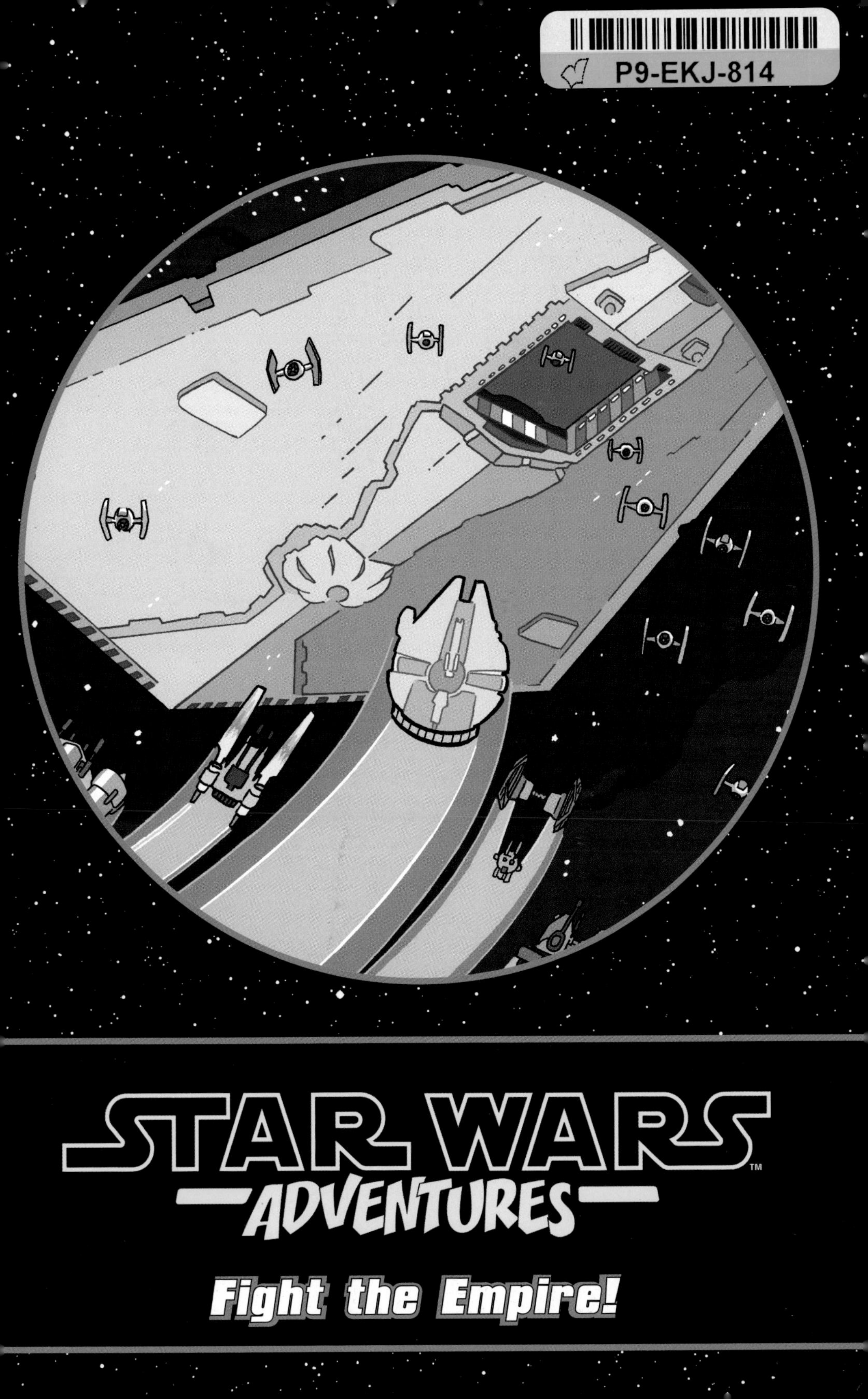

STAR WARS™ ADVENTURES

Fight the Empire!

Facebook: **facebook.com/idwpublishing**
Twitter: **@idwpublishing**
YouTube: **youtube.com/idwpublishing**
Tumblr: **tumblr.idwpublishing.com**
Instagram: **instagram.com/idwpublishing**

ISBN: 978-1-68405-674-3   23 22 21 20   1 2 3 4

COVER ARTIST
ELSA CHARRETIER

COVER COLORIST
SARAH STERN

LETTERER
TOM B. LONG

SERIES ASSISTANT EDITOR
ELIZABETH BREI

Originally published as STAR WARS ADVENTURES issues #21–23.

SERIES EDITOR
DENTON J. TIPTON

Chris Ryall, President & Publisher/CCO
Cara Morrison, Chief Financial Officer
Matthew Ruzicka, Chief Accounting Officer
David Hedgecock, Associate Publisher
John Barber, Editor-in-Chief
Justin Eisinger, Editorial Director, Graphic Novels and Collections
Jerry Bennington, VP of New Product Development
Lorelei Bunjes, VP of Technology & Information Services
Jud Meyers, Sales Director
Anna Morrow, Marketing Director
Tara McCrillis, Director of Design & Production
Mike Ford, Director of Operations
Shauna Monteforte, Manufacturing Operations Director
Rebekah Cahalin, General Manager

Ted Adams and Robbie Robbins, IDW Founders

COLLECTION EDITORS
ALONZO SIMON
& ZAC BOONE

COLLECTION DESIGNER
CLYDE GRAPA

Lucasfilm Credits:
Robert Simpson, Senior Editor
Michael Siglain, Creative Director
Phil Szostak, Lucasfilm Art Department
Matt Martin, Pablo Hidalgo, and
Emily Shkoukani, Story Group

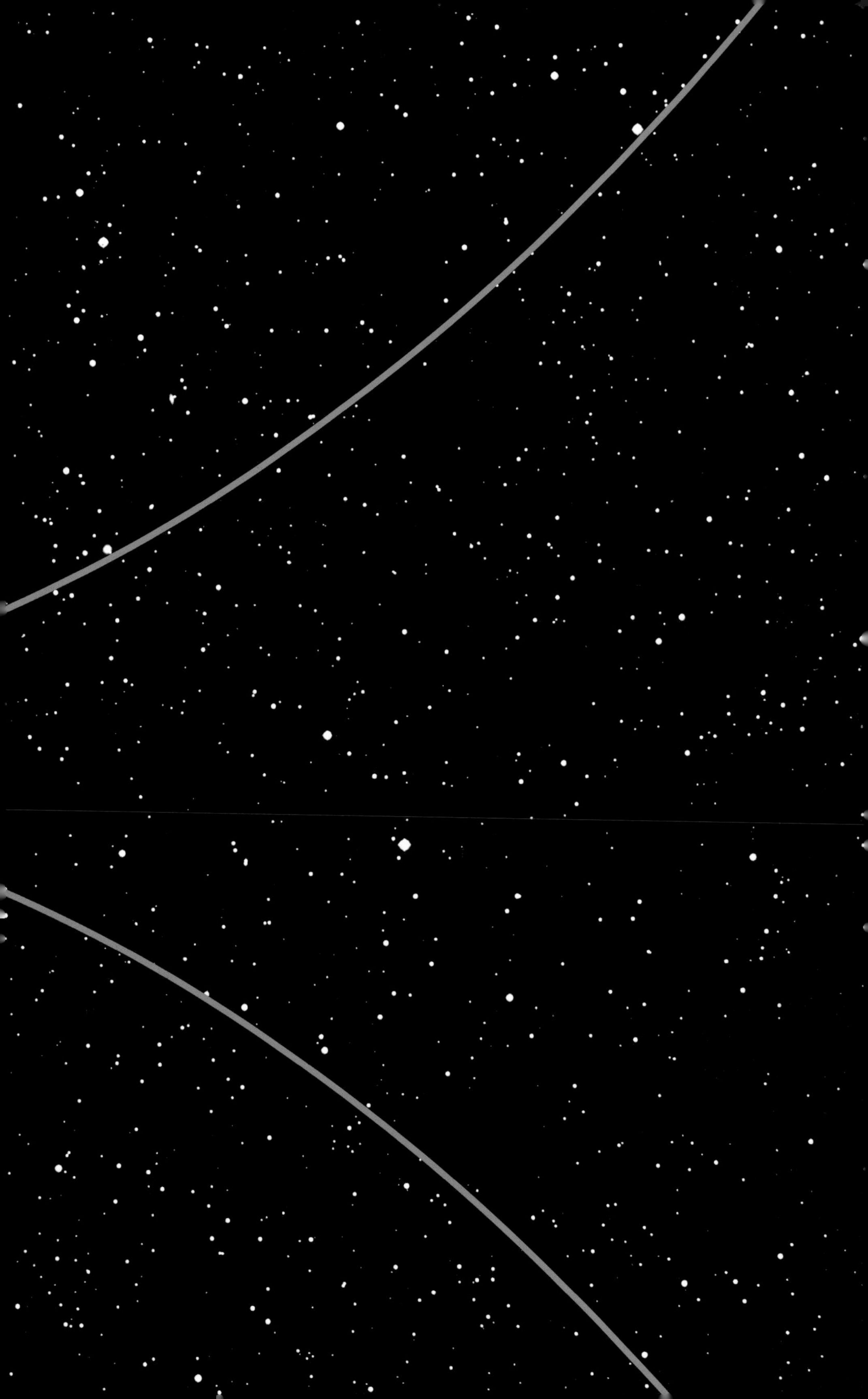

STAR WARS
ADVENTURES

Swoop Racers

WRITER
CAVAN SCOTT

ARTIST
DEREK CHARM

COLORIST
MATT HERMS

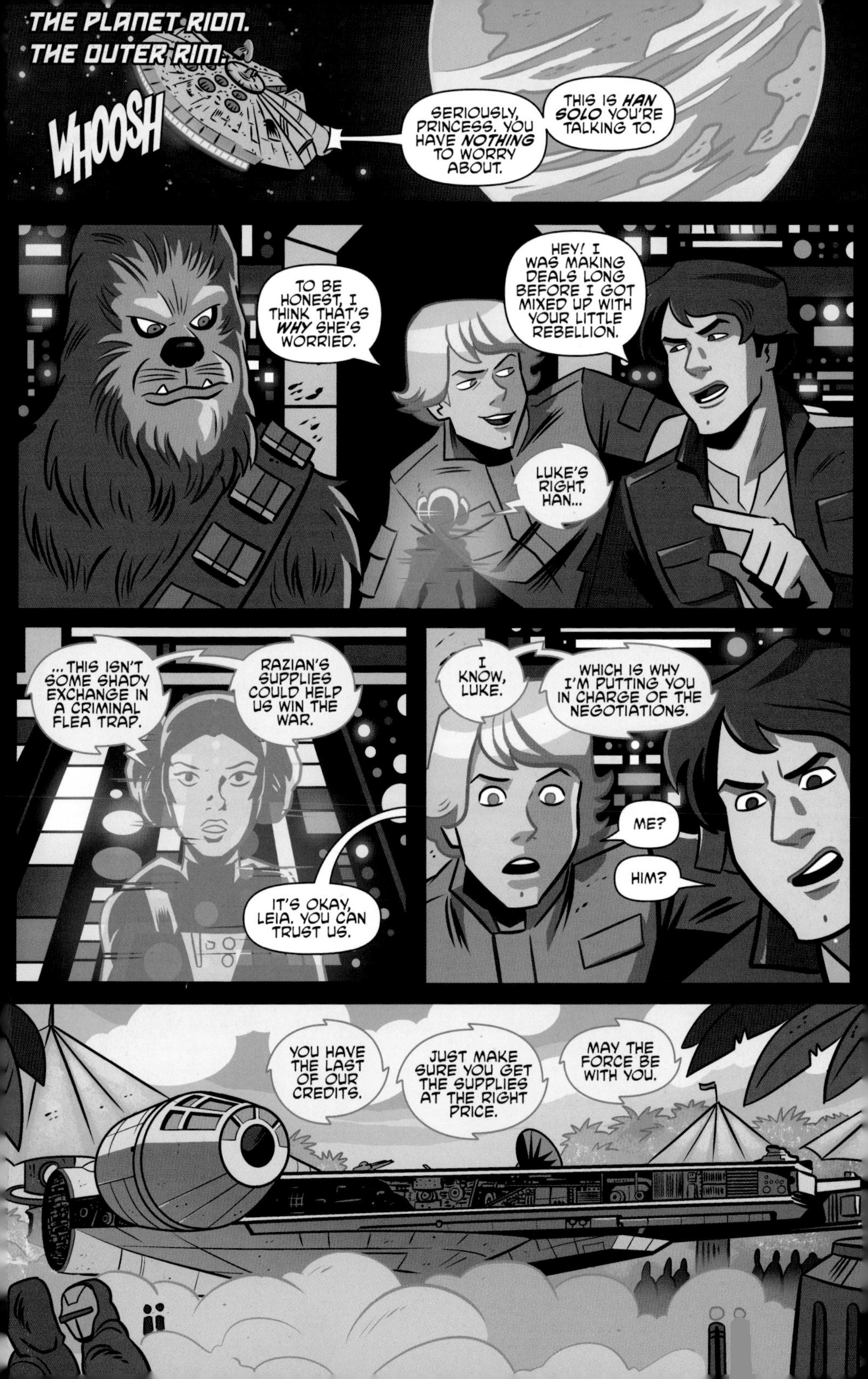
THE PLANET RION. THE OUTER RIM.
WHOOSH
SERIOUSLY, PRINCESS. YOU HAVE NOTHING TO WORRY ABOUT.
THIS IS HAN SOLO YOU'RE TALKING TO.
TO BE HONEST, I THINK THAT'S WHY SHE'S WORRIED.
HEY! I WAS MAKING DEALS LONG BEFORE I GOT MIXED UP WITH YOUR LITTLE REBELLION.
LUKE'S RIGHT, HAN...
...THIS ISN'T SOME SHADY EXCHANGE IN A CRIMINAL FLEA TRAP.
RAZIAN'S SUPPLIES COULD HELP US WIN THE WAR.
IT'S OKAY, LEIA. YOU CAN TRUST US.
I KNOW, LUKE.
WHICH IS WHY I'M PUTTING YOU IN CHARGE OF THE NEGOTIATIONS.
ME?
HIM?
YOU HAVE THE LAST OF OUR CREDITS.
JUST MAKE SURE YOU GET THE SUPPLIES AT THE RIGHT PRICE.
MAY THE FORCE BE WITH YOU.

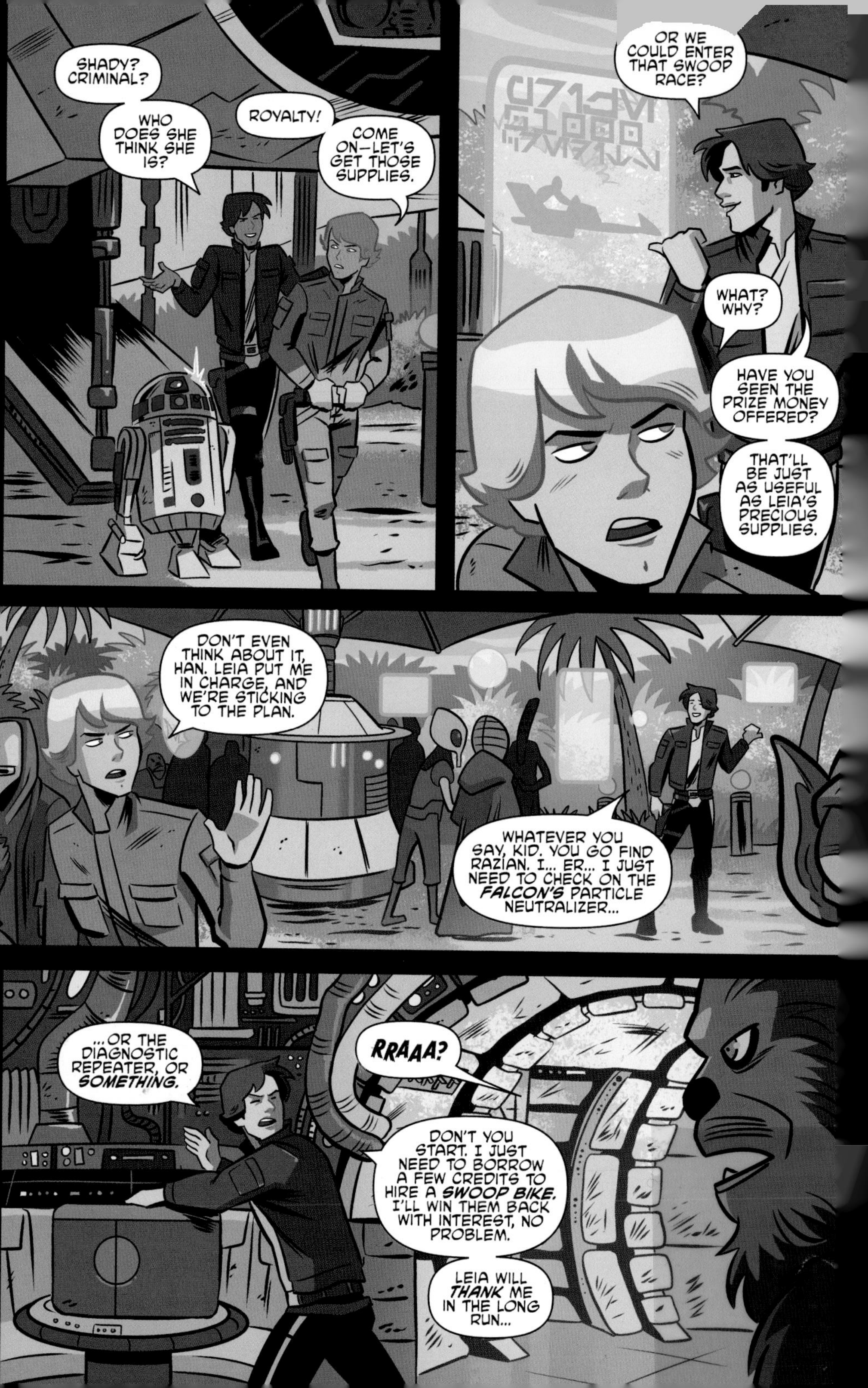
SHADY? CRIMINAL?
WHO DOES SHE THINK SHE IS?
ROYALTY!
COME ON—LET'S GET THOSE SUPPLIES.
OR WE COULD ENTER THAT SWOOP RACE?
WHAT? WHY?
HAVE YOU SEEN THE PRIZE MONEY OFFERED?
THAT'LL BE JUST AS USEFUL AS LEIA'S PRECIOUS SUPPLIES.
DON'T EVEN THINK ABOUT IT, HAN. LEIA PUT ME IN CHARGE, AND WE'RE STICKING TO THE PLAN.
WHATEVER YOU SAY, KID. YOU GO FIND RAZIAN. I... ER... I JUST NEED TO CHECK ON THE *FALCON'S* PARTICLE NEUTRALIZER...
...OR THE DIAGNOSTIC REPEATER, OR *SOMETHING.*
RRAAA?
DON'T YOU START. I JUST NEED TO BORROW A FEW CREDITS TO HIRE A *SWOOP BIKE.* I'LL WIN THEM BACK WITH INTEREST, NO PROBLEM.
LEIA WILL *THANK* ME IN THE LONG RUN...

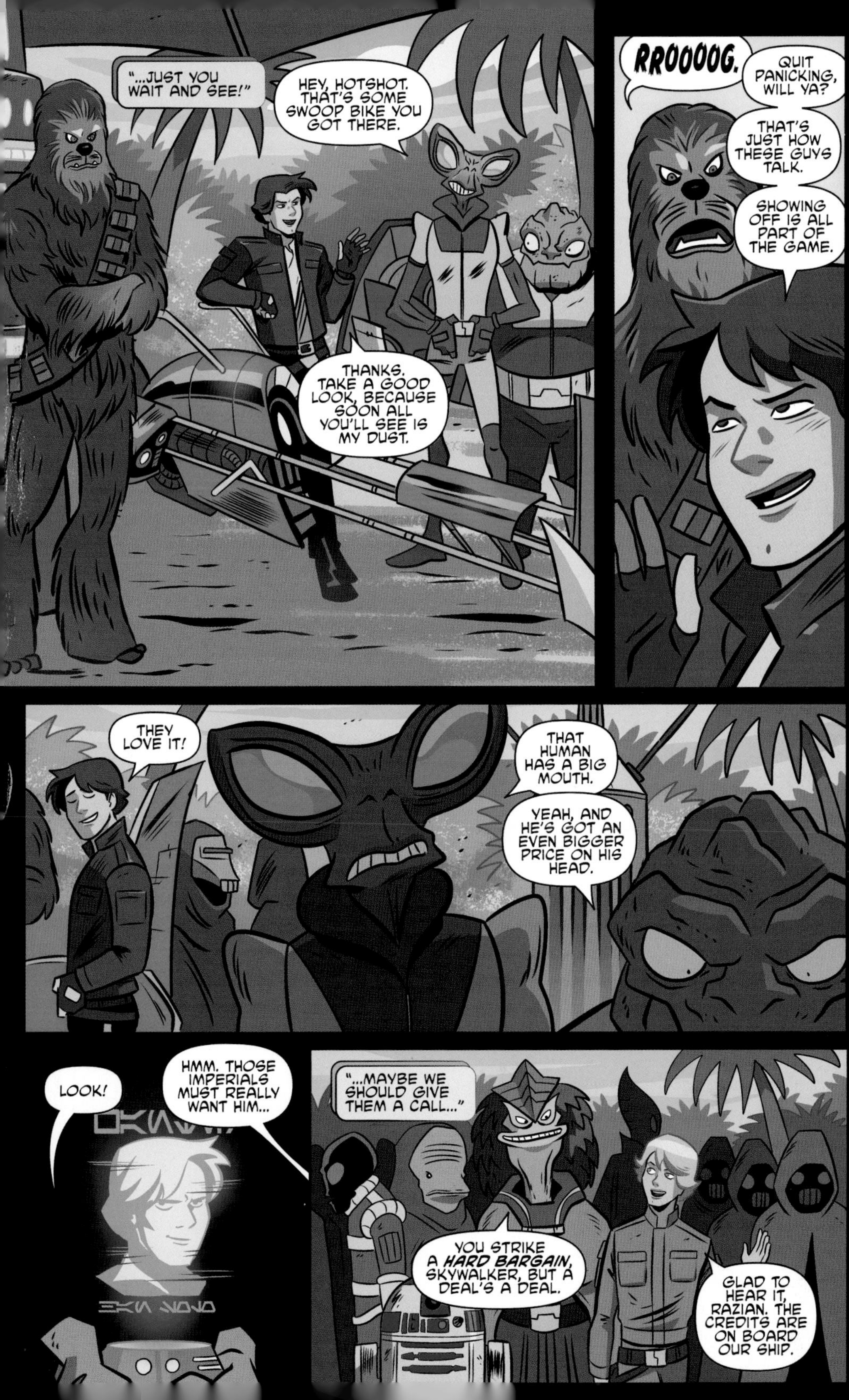
"...JUST YOU WAIT AND SEE!"
HEY, HOTSHOT. THAT'S SOME SWOOP BIKE YOU GOT THERE.
THANKS. TAKE A GOOD LOOK, BECAUSE SOON ALL YOU'LL SEE IS MY DUST.
RROOOOG.
QUIT PANICKING, WILL YA?
THAT'S JUST HOW THESE GUYS TALK.
SHOWING OFF IS ALL PART OF THE GAME.
THEY LOVE IT!
THAT HUMAN HAS A BIG MOUTH.
YEAH, AND HE'S GOT AN EVEN BIGGER PRICE ON HIS HEAD.
LOOK!
HMM. THOSE IMPERIALS MUST REALLY WANT HIM...
"...MAYBE WE SHOULD GIVE THEM A CALL..."
YOU STRIKE A *HARD BARGAIN*, SKYWALKER, BUT A DEAL'S A DEAL.
GLAD TO HEAR IT, RAZIAN. THE CREDITS ARE ON BOARD OUR SHIP.

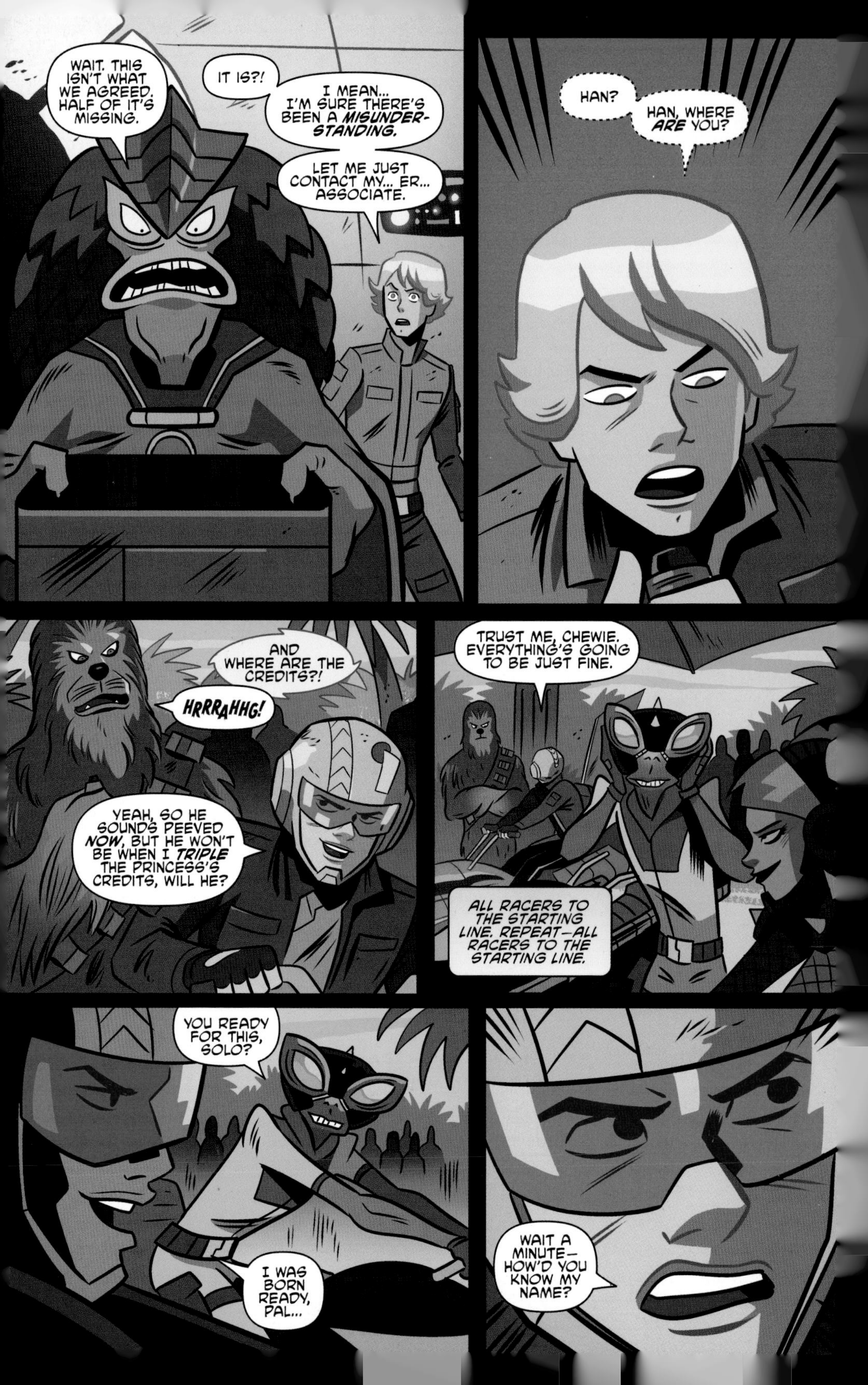
WAIT. THIS ISN'T WHAT WE AGREED. HALF OF IT'S MISSING.
IT IS?!
I MEAN... I'M SURE THERE'S BEEN A *MISUNDERSTANDING.*
LET ME JUST CONTACT MY... ER... ASSOCIATE.
HAN?
HAN, WHERE *ARE* YOU?
AND WHERE ARE THE CREDITS?!
HRRRAHHG!
YEAH, SO HE SOUNDS PEEVED *NOW*, BUT HE WON'T BE WHEN I *TRIPLE* THE PRINCESS'S CREDITS, WILL HE?
TRUST ME, CHEWIE. EVERYTHING'S GOING TO BE JUST FINE.
ALL RACERS TO THE STARTING LINE. REPEAT—ALL RACERS TO THE STARTING LINE.
YOU READY FOR THIS, SOLO?
I WAS BORN READY, PAL...
WAIT A MINUTE—HOW'D YOU KNOW MY NAME?

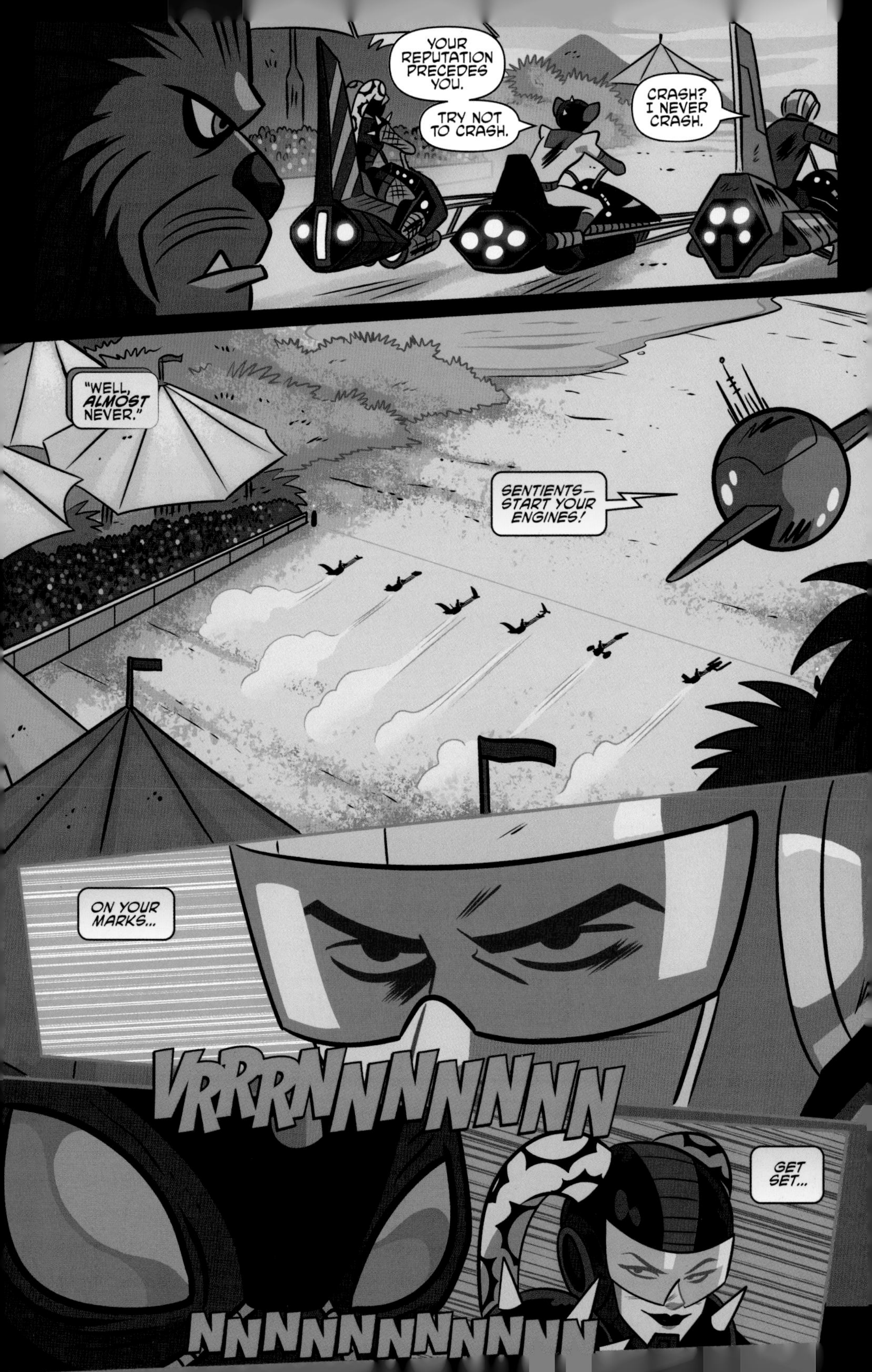
YOUR REPUTATION PRECEDES YOU.
TRY NOT TO CRASH.
CRASH? I NEVER CRASH.
"WELL, ALMOST NEVER."
SENTIENTS-START YOUR ENGINES!
ON YOUR MARKS...
VRRRNNNNNNNN
GET SET...
NNNNNNNNNNNNN

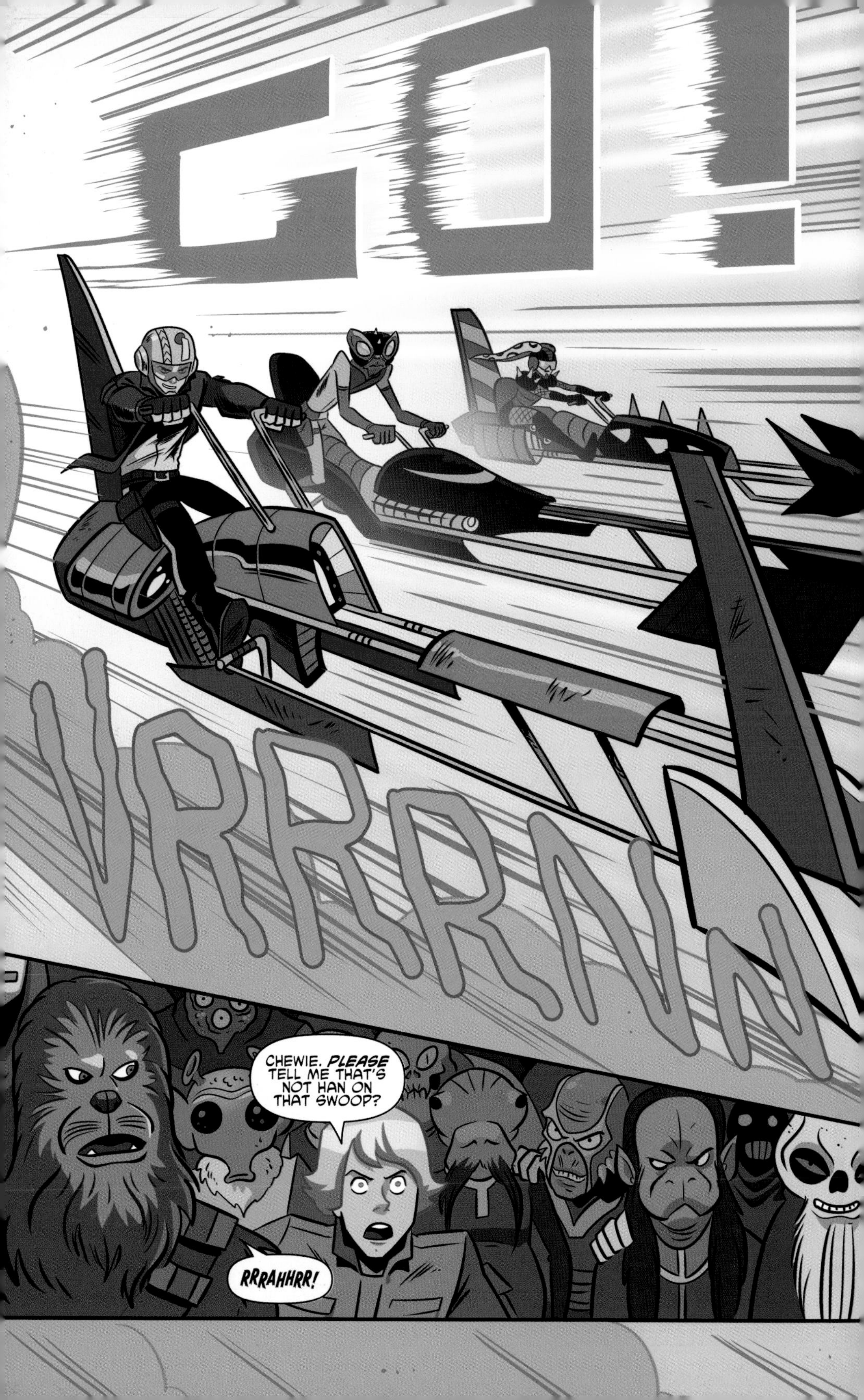
GO!
VRRRMM
CHEWIE. PLEASE TELL ME THAT'S NOT HAN ON THAT SWOOP?
RRRAHHRR!

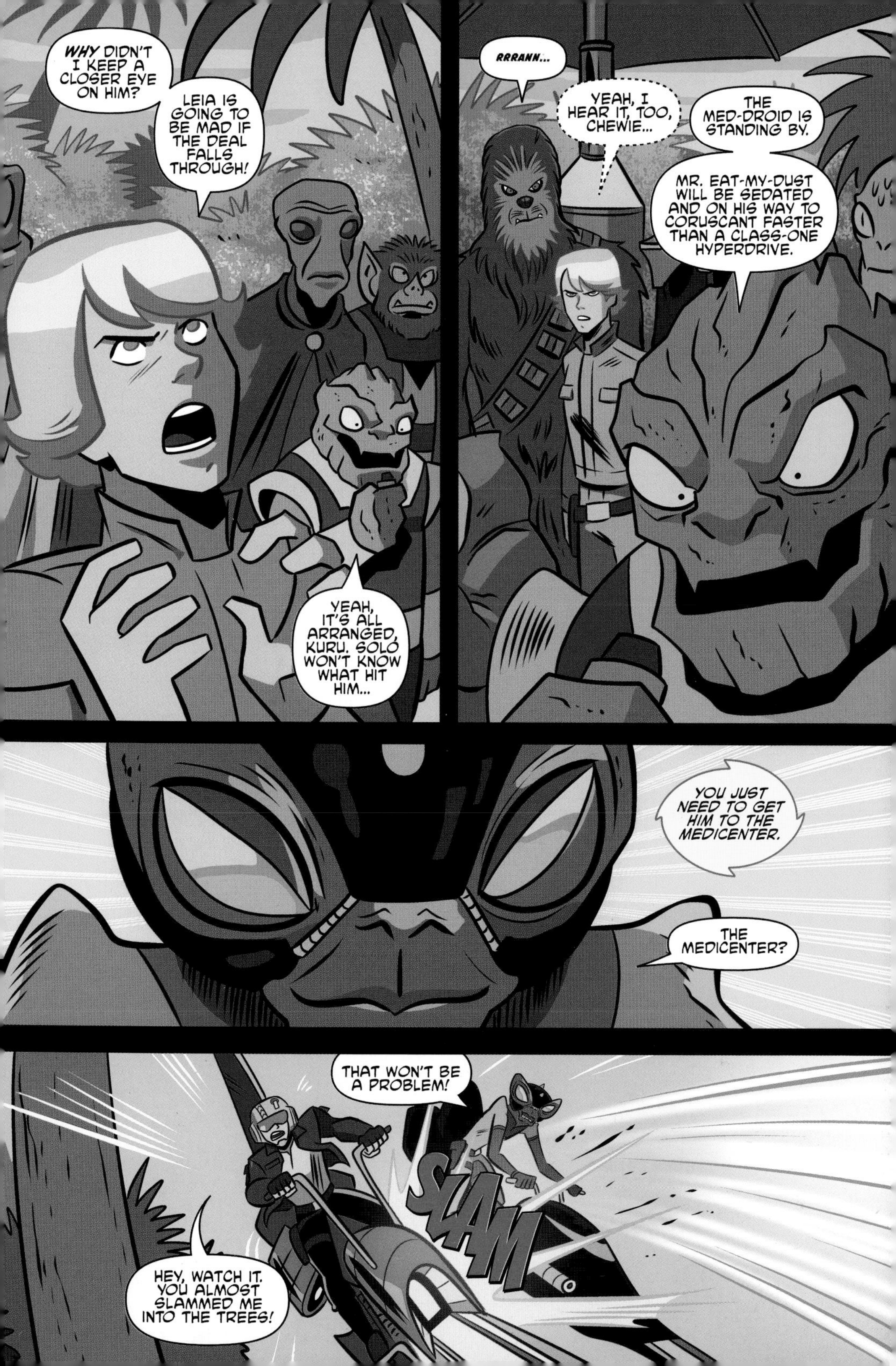

WHY DIDN'T I KEEP A CLOSER EYE ON HIM?
LEIA IS GOING TO BE MAD IF THE DEAL FALLS THROUGH!
YEAH, IT'S ALL ARRANGED, KURU. SOLO WON'T KNOW WHAT HIT HIM...
RRRANN...
YEAH, I HEAR IT, TOO, CHEWIE...
THE MED-DROID IS STANDING BY.
MR. EAT-MY-DUST WILL BE SEDATED AND ON HIS WAY TO CORUSCANT FASTER THAN A CLASS-ONE HYPERDRIVE.
YOU JUST NEED TO GET HIM TO THE MEDICENTER.
THE MEDICENTER?
THAT WON'T BE A PROBLEM!
SLAM
HEY, WATCH IT. YOU ALMOST SLAMMED ME INTO THE TREES!

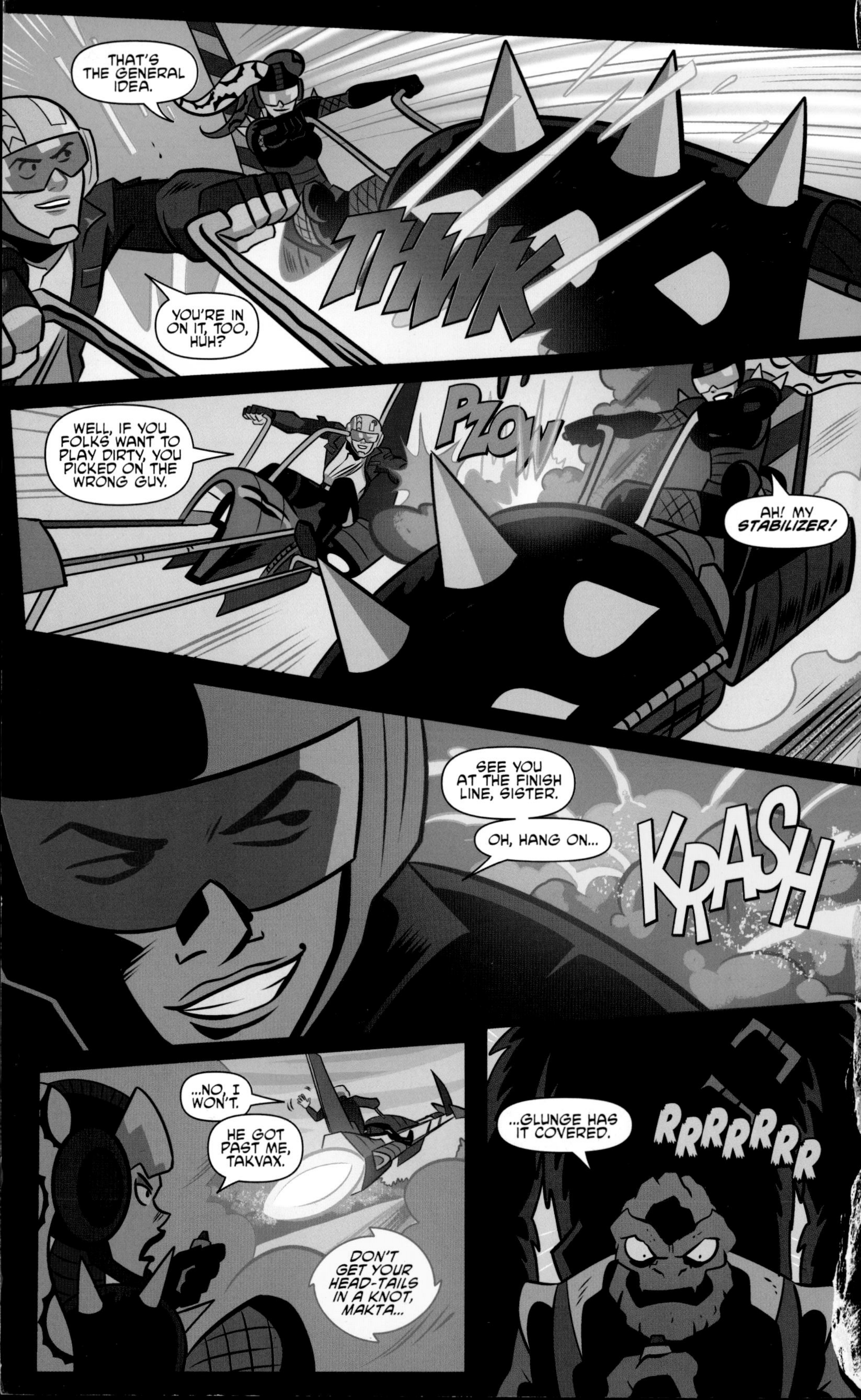

THAT'S THE GENERAL IDEA.
THWK
YOU'RE IN ON IT, TOO, HUH?
WELL, IF YOU FOLKS WANT TO PLAY DIRTY, YOU PICKED ON THE WRONG GUY.
PZOW
AH! MY STABILIZER!
SEE YOU AT THE FINISH LINE, SISTER.
OH, HANG ON...
KRASH
...NO, I WON'T.
HE GOT PAST ME, TAKVAX.
DON'T GET YOUR HEAD-TAILS IN A KNOT, MAKTA...
...GLUNGE HAS IT COVERED.
RRRRRRR

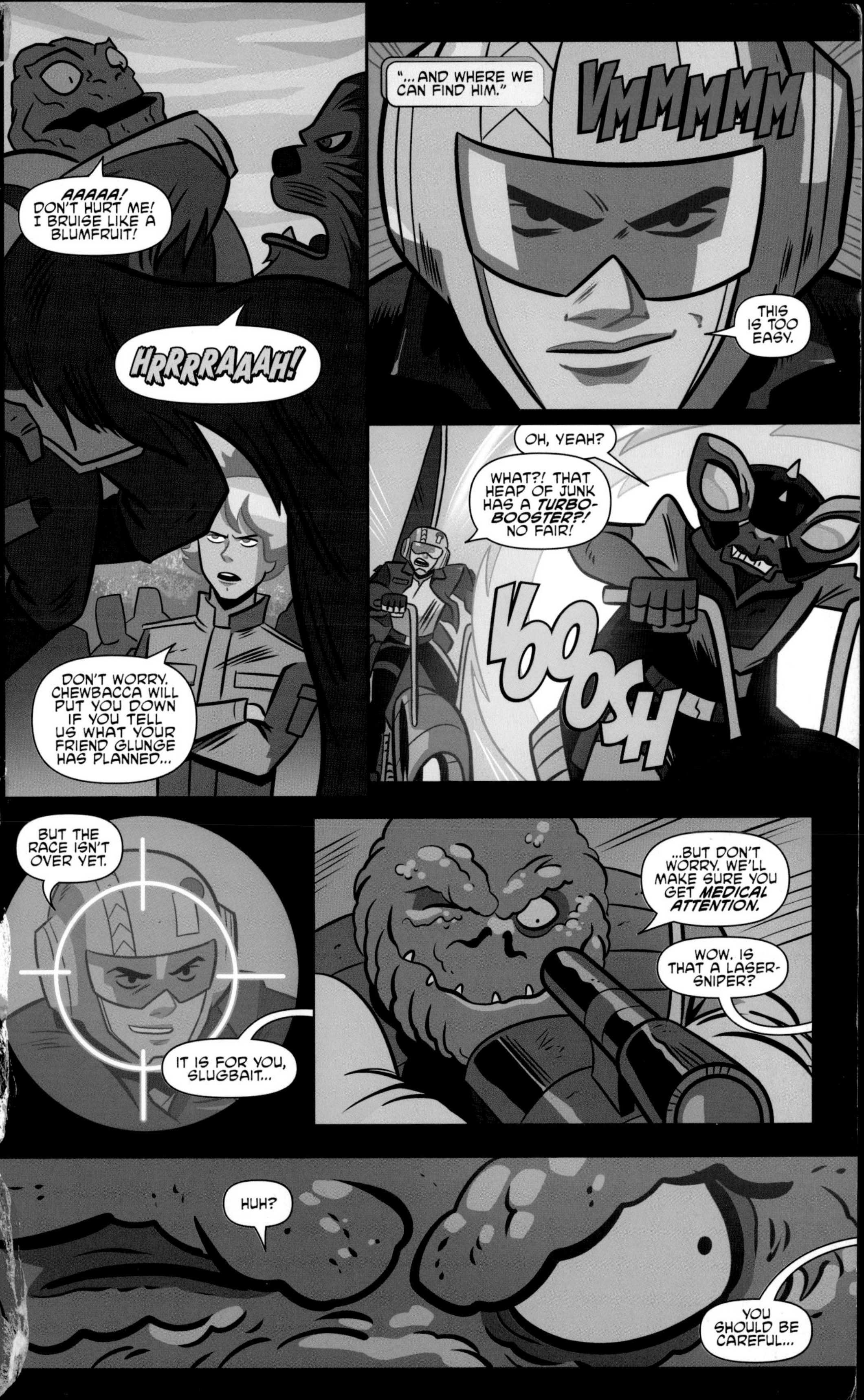
AAAAA! DON'T HURT ME! I BRUISE LIKE A BLUMFRUIT!
HRRRRAAAH!
DON'T WORRY. CHEWBACCA WILL PUT YOU DOWN IF YOU TELL US WHAT YOUR FRIEND GLUNGE HAS PLANNED...
"...AND WHERE WE CAN FIND HIM."
VMMMMMM
THIS IS TOO EASY.
OH, YEAH?
WHAT?! THAT HEAP OF JUNK HAS A TURBO-BOOSTER?! NO FAIR!
VOOOOSH
BUT THE RACE ISN'T OVER YET.
IT IS FOR YOU, SLUGBAIT...
...BUT DON'T WORRY. WE'LL MAKE SURE YOU GET MEDICAL ATTENTION.
WOW. IS THAT A LASER-SNIPER?
HUH?
YOU SHOULD BE CAREFUL...

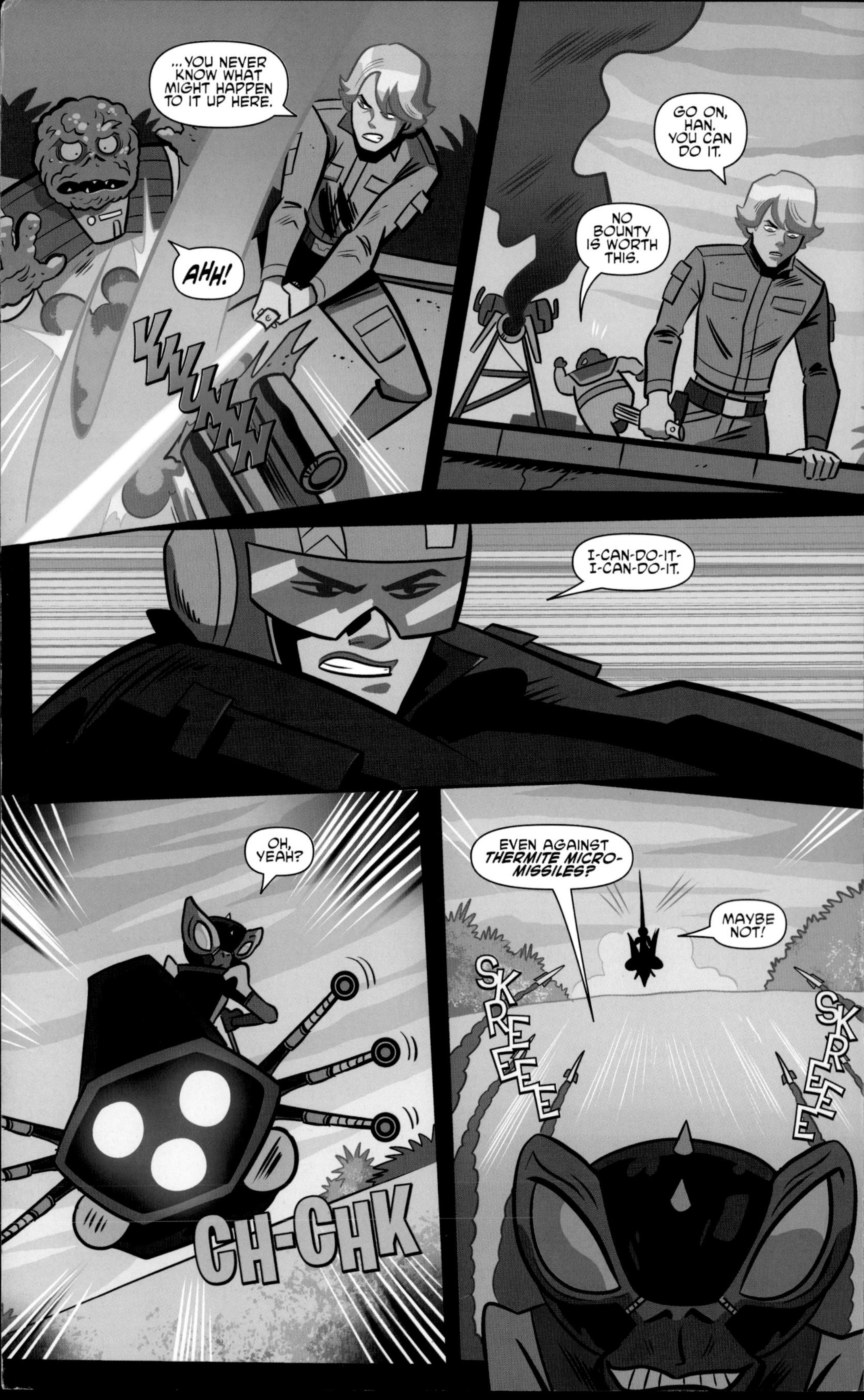
...YOU NEVER KNOW WHAT MIGHT HAPPEN TO IT UP HERE.
AHH!
VVVUNNNN
GO ON, HAN. YOU CAN DO IT.
NO BOUNTY IS WORTH THIS.
I-CAN-DO-IT-I-CAN-DO-IT.
OH, YEAH?
CH-CHK
EVEN AGAINST *THERMITE MICRO-MISSILES?*
MAYBE NOT!
SKREEEE
SKREEEE

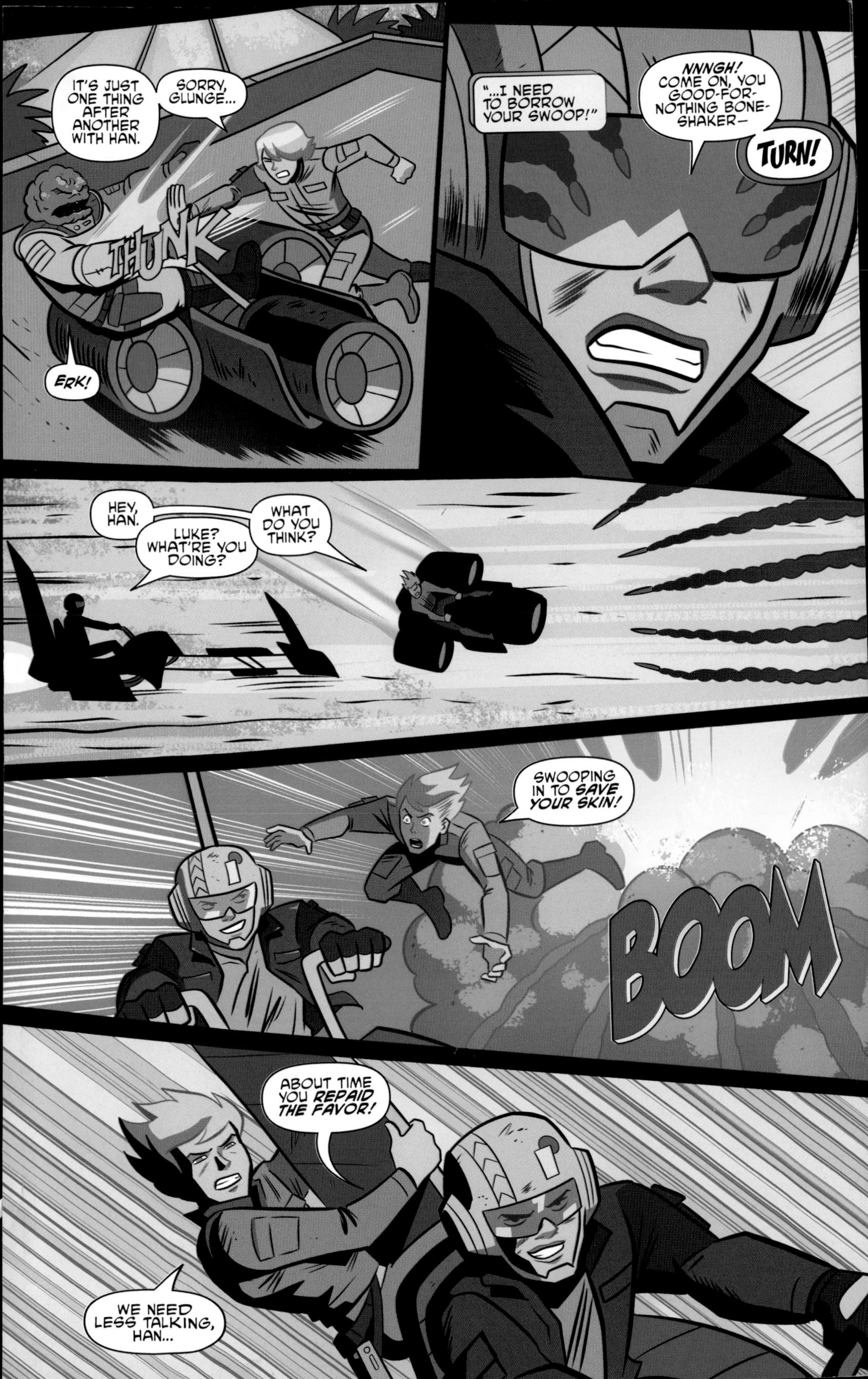
IT'S JUST ONE THING AFTER ANOTHER WITH HAN.
SORRY, GLUNGE...
THUNK
ERK!
"...I NEED TO BORROW YOUR SWOOP!"
NNNGH! COME ON, YOU GOOD-FOR-NOTHING BONE-SHAKER—
TURN!
HEY, HAN.
LUKE? WHAT'RE YOU DOING?
WHAT DO YOU THINK?
SWOOPING IN TO SAVE YOUR SKIN!
BOOM
ABOUT TIME YOU REPAID THE FAVOR!
WE NEED LESS TALKING, HAN...

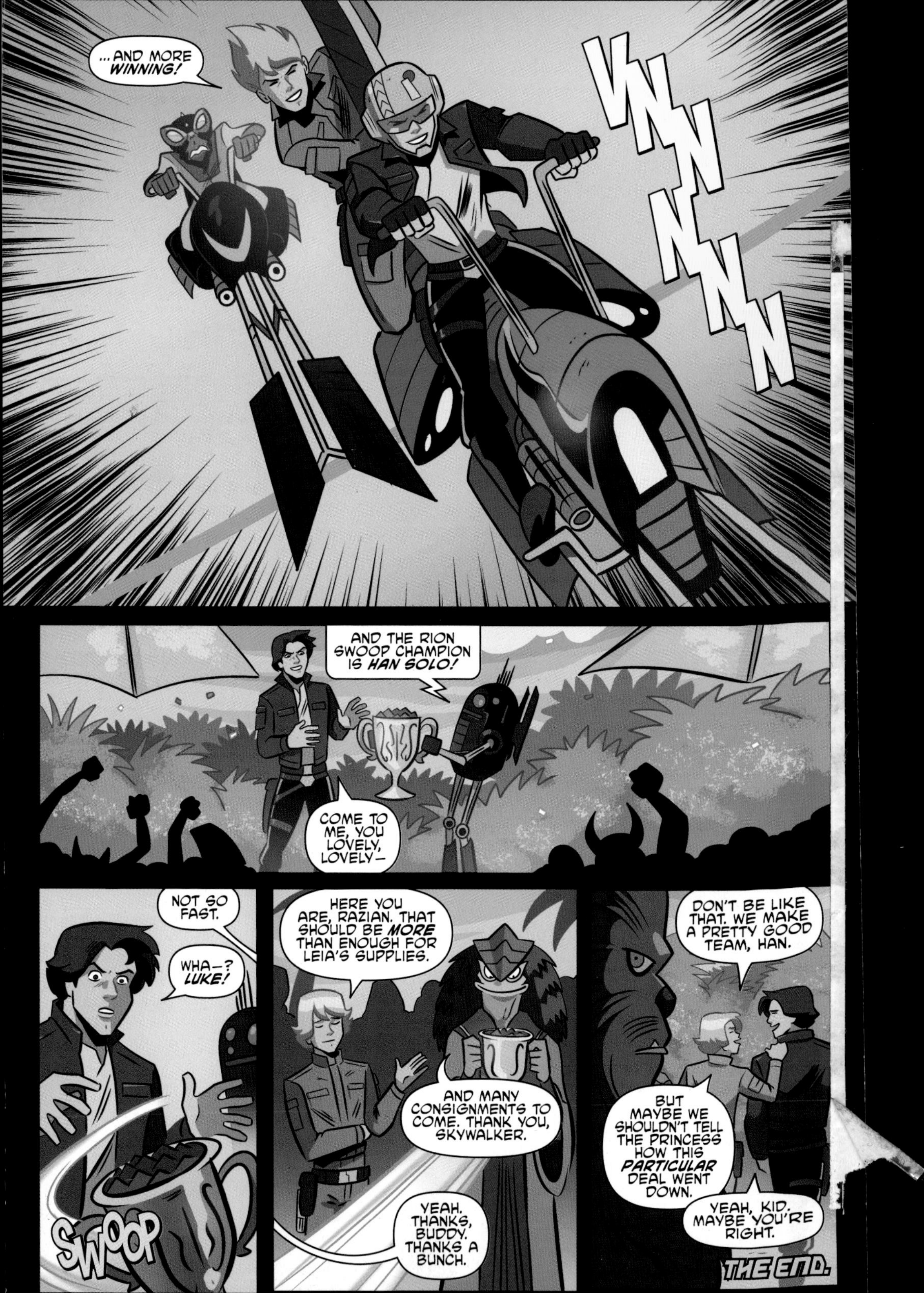
...AND MORE WINNING!
VNNNNNNN
AND THE RION SWOOP CHAMPION IS HAN SOLO!
COME TO ME, YOU LOVELY, LOVELY—
NOT SO FAST.
WHA—? LUKE!
SWOOP
HERE YOU ARE, RAZIAN. THAT SHOULD BE MORE THAN ENOUGH FOR LEIA'S SUPPLIES.
AND MANY CONSIGNMENTS TO COME. THANK YOU, SKYWALKER.
YEAH. THANKS, BUDDY. THANKS A BUNCH.
DON'T BE LIKE THAT. WE MAKE A PRETTY GOOD TEAM, HAN.
BUT MAYBE WE SHOULDN'T TELL THE PRINCESS HOW THIS PARTICULAR DEAL WENT DOWN.
YEAH, KID. MAYBE YOU'RE RIGHT.
THE END.

STAR WARS ™
—ADVENTURES—

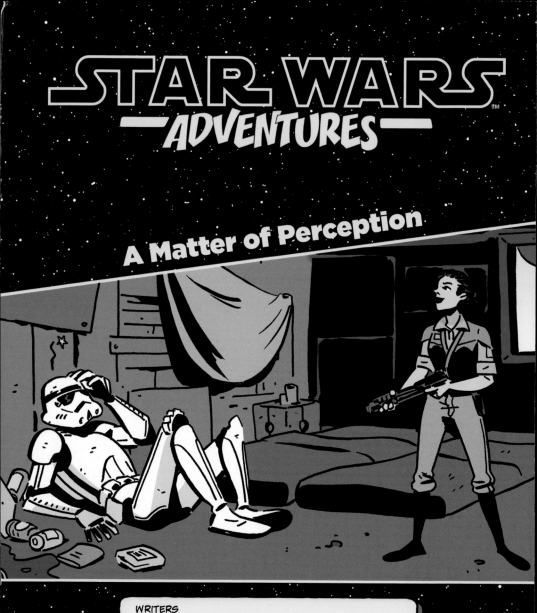

A Matter of Perception

WRITERS
PIERRICK COLINET & ELSA CHARRETIER

ARTIST
ELSA CHARRETIER

COLORIST
SARAH STERN

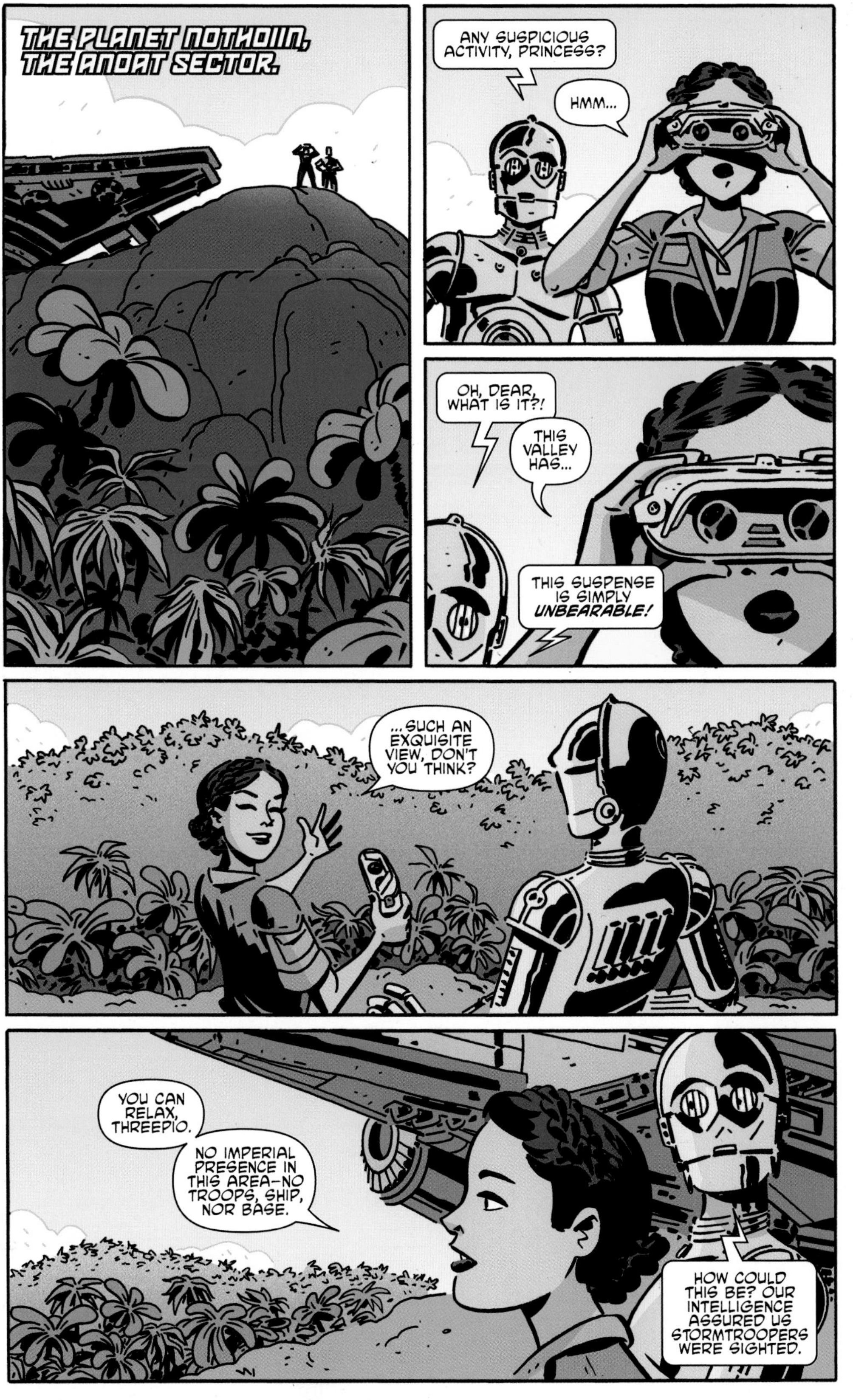
THE PLANET NOTHOIIN, THE ANOAT SECTOR.
ANY SUSPICIOUS ACTIVITY, PRINCESS?
HMM...
OH, DEAR, WHAT IS IT?!
THIS VALLEY HAS...
THIS SUSPENSE IS SIMPLY *UNBEARABLE!*
...SUCH AN EXQUISITE VIEW, DON'T YOU THINK?
YOU CAN RELAX, THREEPIO.
NO IMPERIAL PRESENCE IN THIS AREA—NO TROOPS, SHIP, NOR BASE.
HOW COULD THIS BE? OUR INTELLIGENCE ASSURED US STORMTROOPERS WERE SIGHTED.

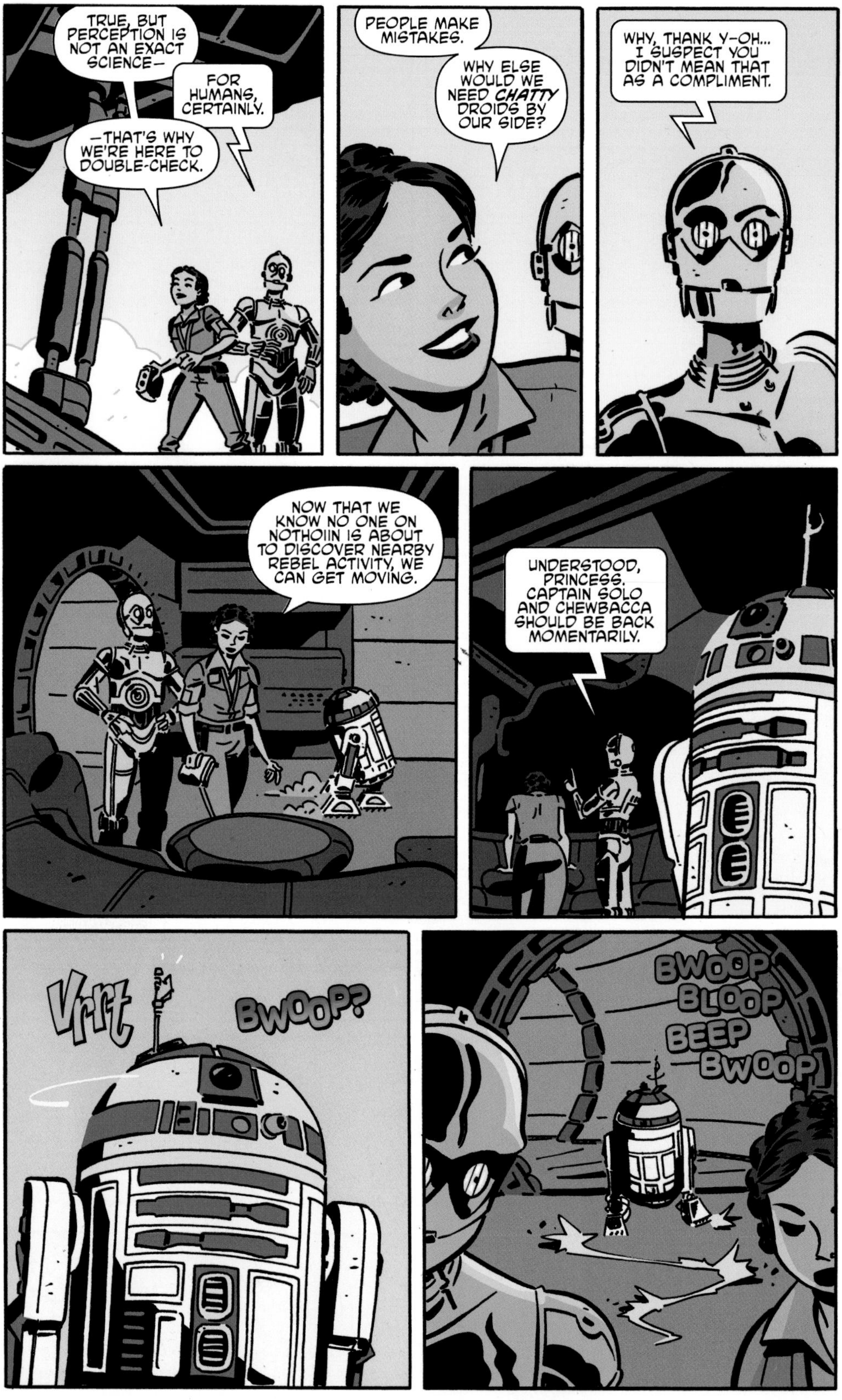
TRUE, BUT PERCEPTION IS NOT AN EXACT SCIENCE—
FOR HUMANS, CERTAINLY.
—THAT'S WHY WE'RE HERE TO DOUBLE-CHECK.
PEOPLE MAKE MISTAKES.
WHY ELSE WOULD WE NEED CHATTY DROIDS BY OUR SIDE?
WHY, THANK Y—OH... I SUSPECT YOU DIDN'T MEAN THAT AS A COMPLIMENT.
NOW THAT WE KNOW NO ONE ON NOTHOIIN IS ABOUT TO DISCOVER NEARBY REBEL ACTIVITY, WE CAN GET MOVING.
UNDERSTOOD, PRINCESS. CAPTAIN SOLO AND CHEWBACCA SHOULD BE BACK MOMENTARILY.
Vrrt
BWOOP?
BWOOP BLOOP BEEP BWOOP

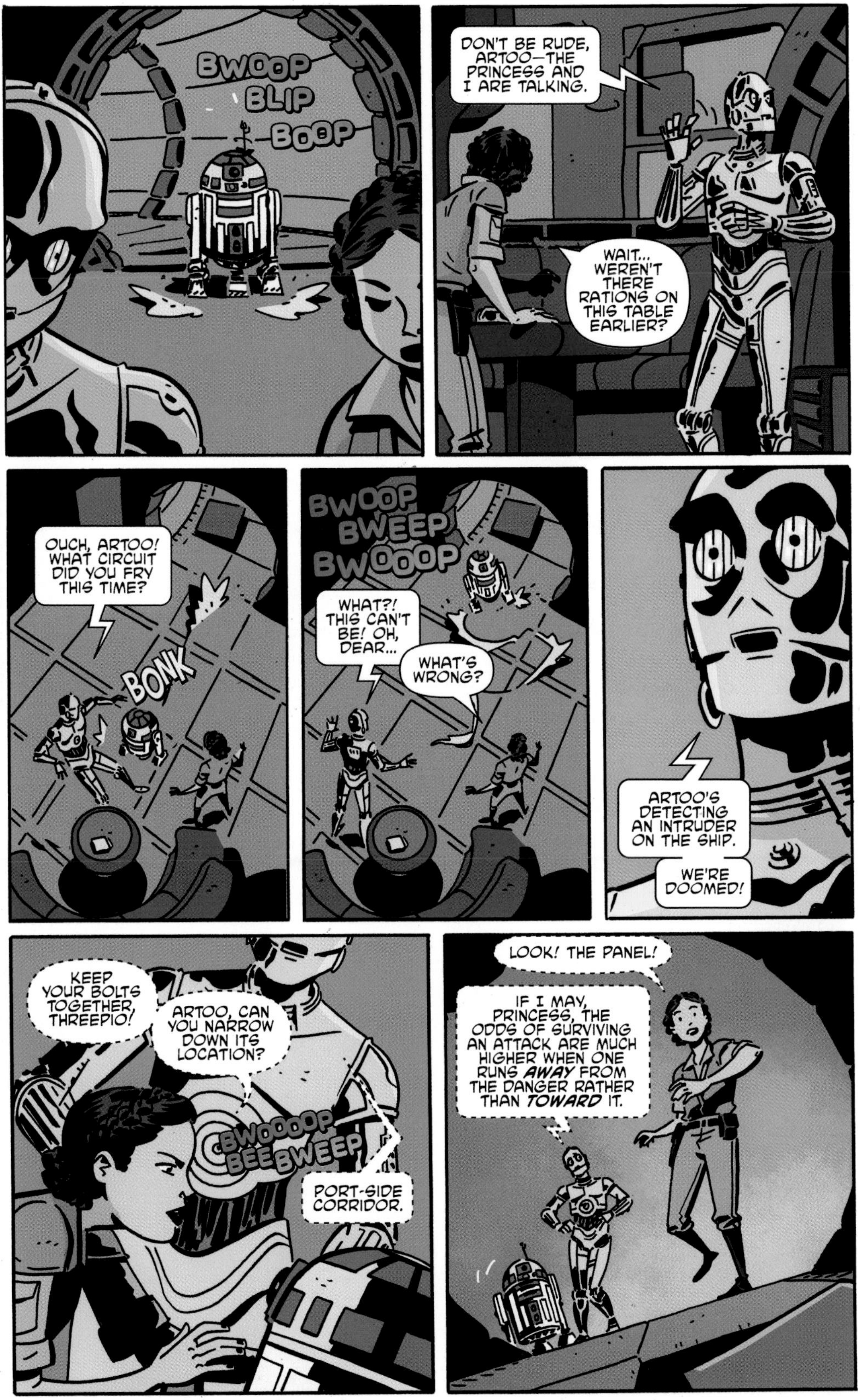
BWOOP
BLIP
BOOP
DON'T BE RUDE, ARTOO—THE PRINCESS AND I ARE TALKING.
WAIT... WEREN'T THERE RATIONS ON THIS TABLE EARLIER?
OUCH, ARTOO! WHAT CIRCUIT DID YOU FRY THIS TIME?
BONK
BWOOP
BWEEP
BWOOOP
WHAT?! THIS CAN'T BE! OH, DEAR...
WHAT'S WRONG?
ARTOO'S DETECTING AN INTRUDER ON THE SHIP.
WE'RE DOOMED!
KEEP YOUR BOLTS TOGETHER, THREEPIO!
ARTOO, CAN YOU NARROW DOWN ITS LOCATION?
BWOOOOP
BEEBWEEP
PORT-SIDE CORRIDOR.
LOOK! THE PANEL!
IF I MAY, PRINCESS, THE ODDS OF SURVIVING AN ATTACK ARE MUCH HIGHER WHEN ONE RUNS AWAY FROM THE DANGER RATHER THAN TOWARD IT.

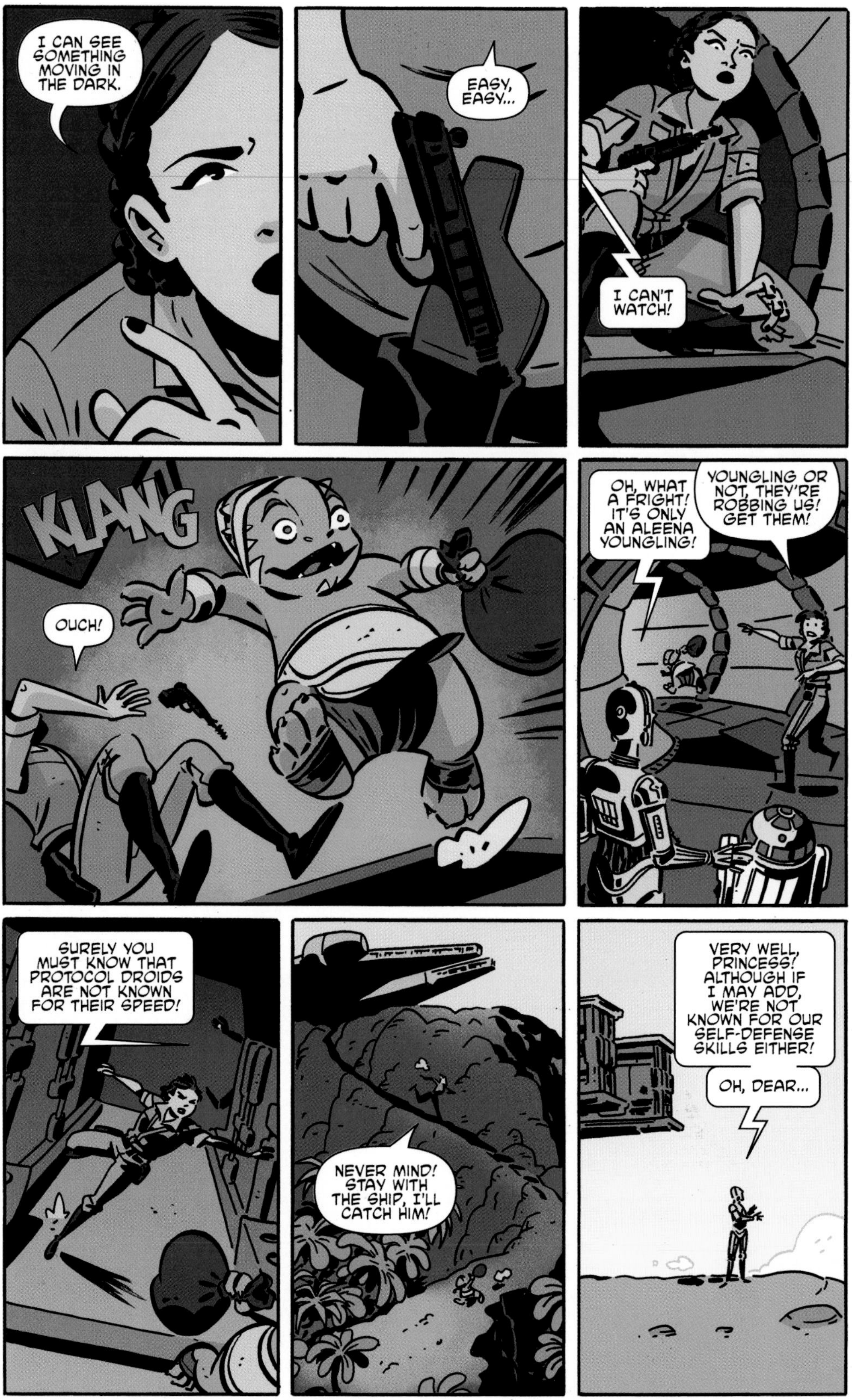
I CAN SEE SOMETHING MOVING IN THE DARK.
EASY, EASY...
I CAN'T WATCH!
KLANG
OUCH!
OH, WHAT A FRIGHT! IT'S ONLY AN ALEENA YOUNGLING!
YOUNGLING OR NOT, THEY'RE ROBBING US! GET THEM!
SURELY YOU MUST KNOW THAT PROTOCOL DROIDS ARE NOT KNOWN FOR THEIR SPEED!
NEVER MIND! STAY WITH THE SHIP, I'LL CATCH HIM!
VERY WELL, PRINCESS! ALTHOUGH IF I MAY ADD, WE'RE NOT KNOWN FOR OUR SELF-DEFENSE SKILLS EITHER!
OH, DEAR...

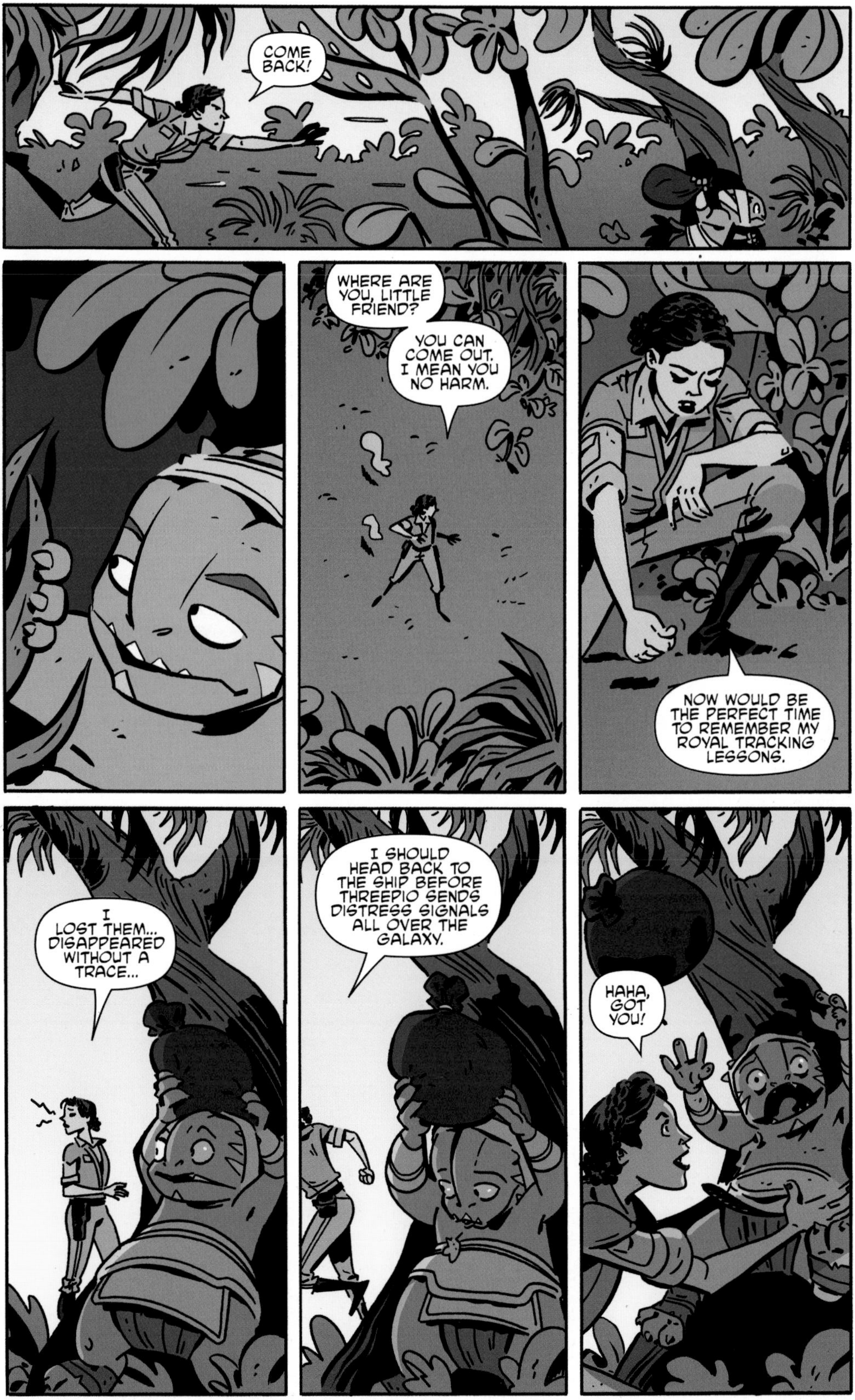
COME BACK!
WHERE ARE YOU, LITTLE FRIEND?
YOU CAN COME OUT. I MEAN YOU NO HARM.
NOW WOULD BE THE PERFECT TIME TO REMEMBER MY ROYAL TRACKING LESSONS.
I LOST THEM... DISAPPEARED WITHOUT A TRACE...
I SHOULD HEAD BACK TO THE SHIP BEFORE THREEPIO SENDS DISTRESS SIGNALS ALL OVER THE GALAXY.
HAHA, GOT YOU!

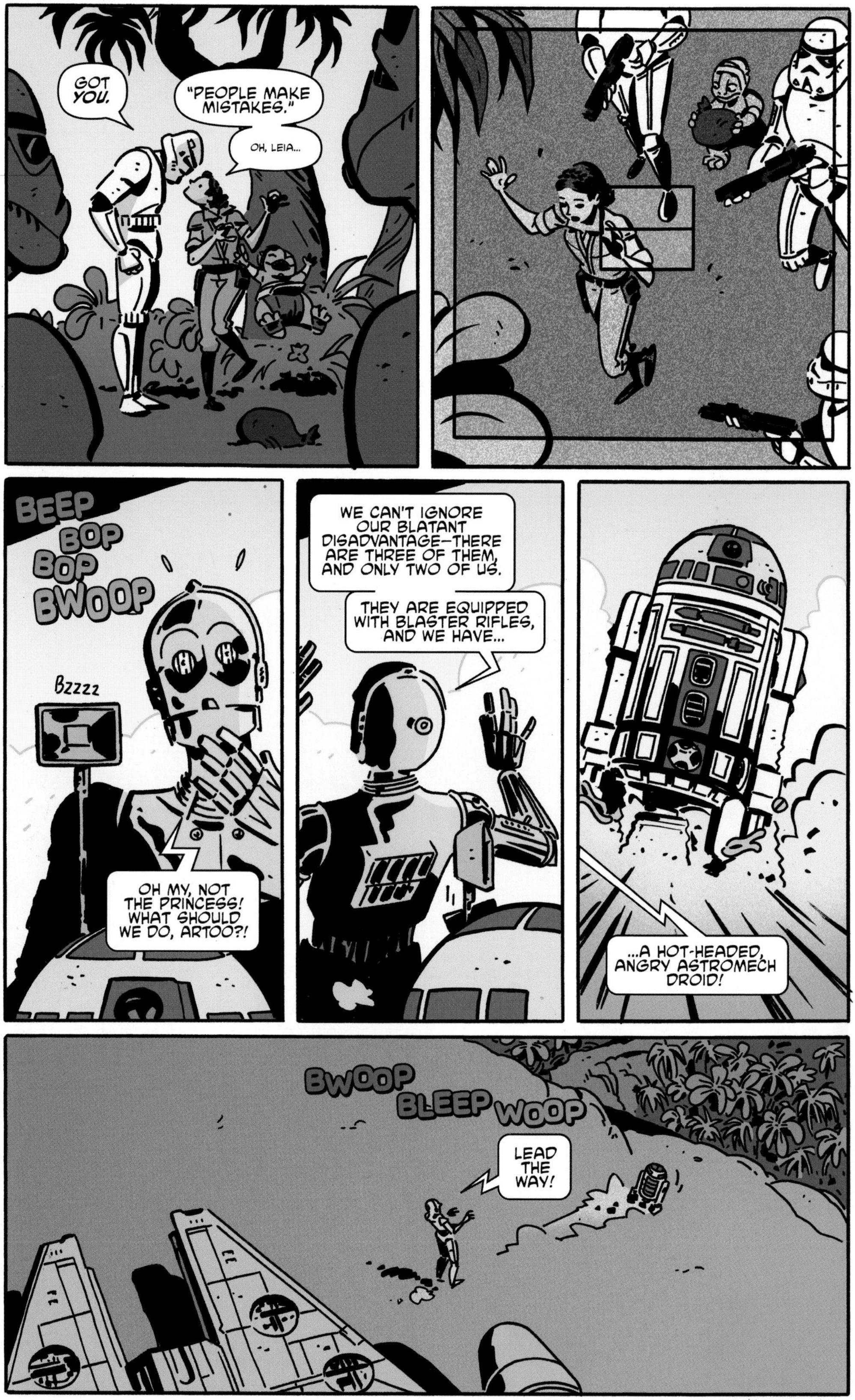
GOT YOU.
"PEOPLE MAKE MISTAKES."
OH, LEIA...
BEEP BOP BOP BWOOP
Bzzzz
OH MY, NOT THE PRINCESS! WHAT SHOULD WE DO, ARTOO?!
WE CAN'T IGNORE OUR BLATANT DISADVANTAGE—THERE ARE THREE OF THEM, AND ONLY TWO OF US.
THEY ARE EQUIPPED WITH BLASTER RIFLES, AND WE HAVE...
...A HOT-HEADED, ANGRY ASTROMECH DROID!
BWOOP BLEEP WOOP
LEAD THE WAY!

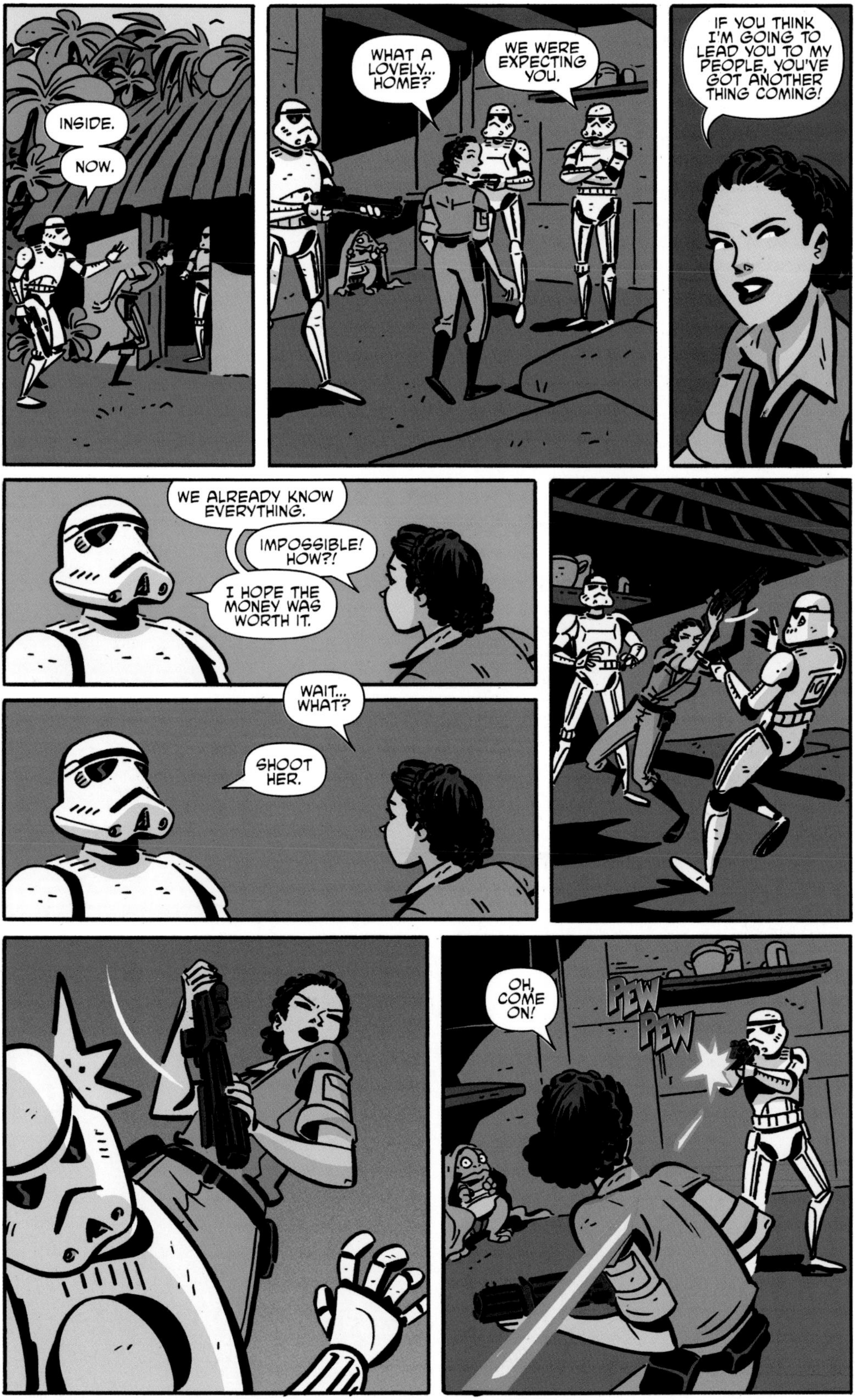
INSIDE.
NOW.
WHAT A LOVELY... HOME?
WE WERE EXPECTING YOU.
IF YOU THINK I'M GOING TO LEAD YOU TO MY PEOPLE, YOU'VE GOT ANOTHER THING COMING!
WE ALREADY KNOW EVERYTHING.
IMPOSSIBLE! HOW?!
I HOPE THE MONEY WAS WORTH IT.
WAIT... WHAT?
SHOOT HER.
OH, COME ON!
PEW
PEW

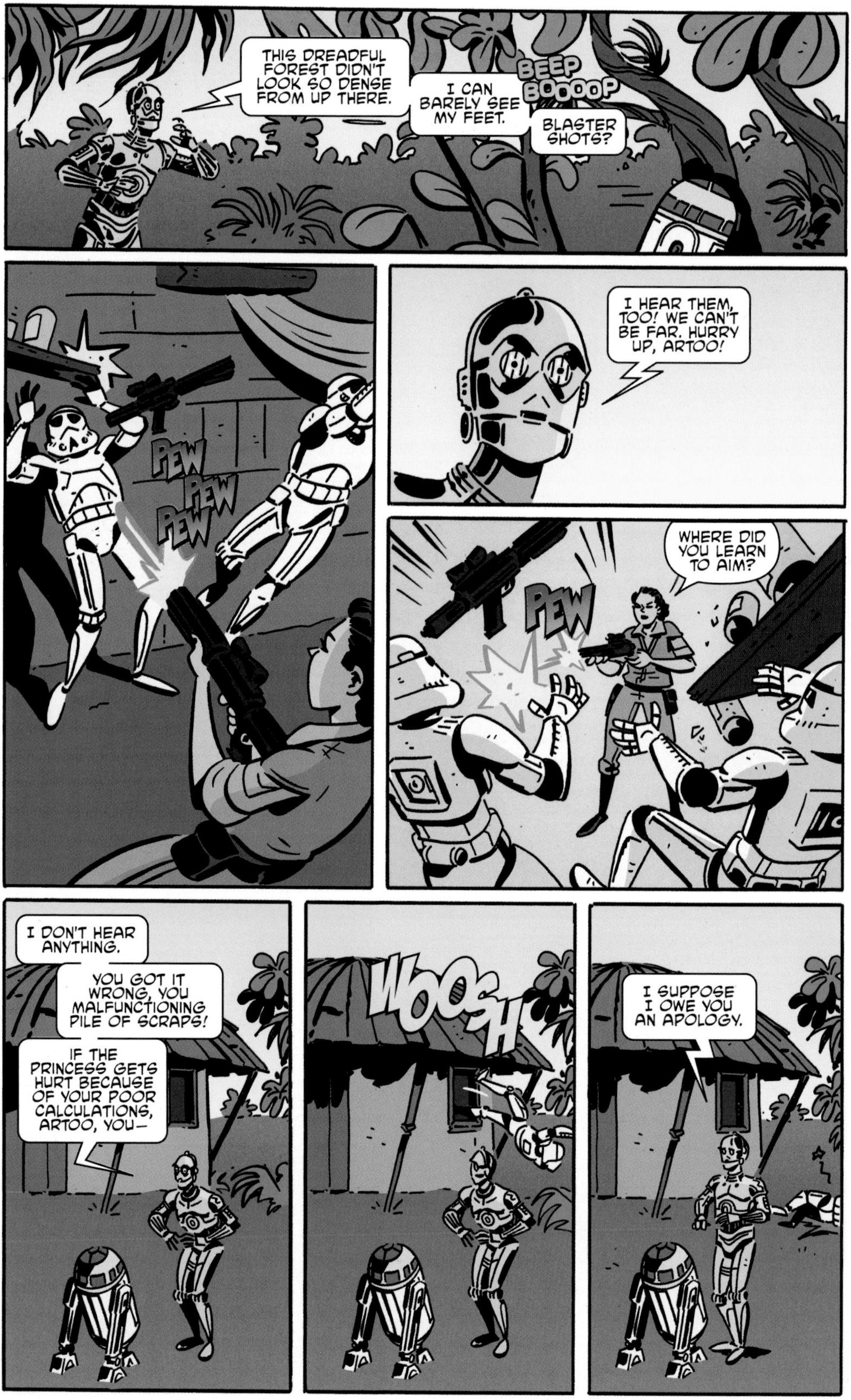
THIS DREADFUL FOREST DIDN'T LOOK SO DENSE FROM UP THERE.
I CAN BARELY SEE MY FEET.
BEEP BOOOOP
BLASTER SHOTS?
PEW PEW PEW
I HEAR THEM, TOO! WE CAN'T BE FAR. HURRY UP, ARTOO!
WHERE DID YOU LEARN TO AIM?
PEW
I DON'T HEAR ANYTHING.
YOU GOT IT WRONG, YOU MALFUNCTIONING PILE OF SCRAPS!
IF THE PRINCESS GETS HURT BECAUSE OF YOUR POOR CALCULATIONS, ARTOO, YOU—
WOOSH
I SUPPOSE I OWE YOU AN APOLOGY.

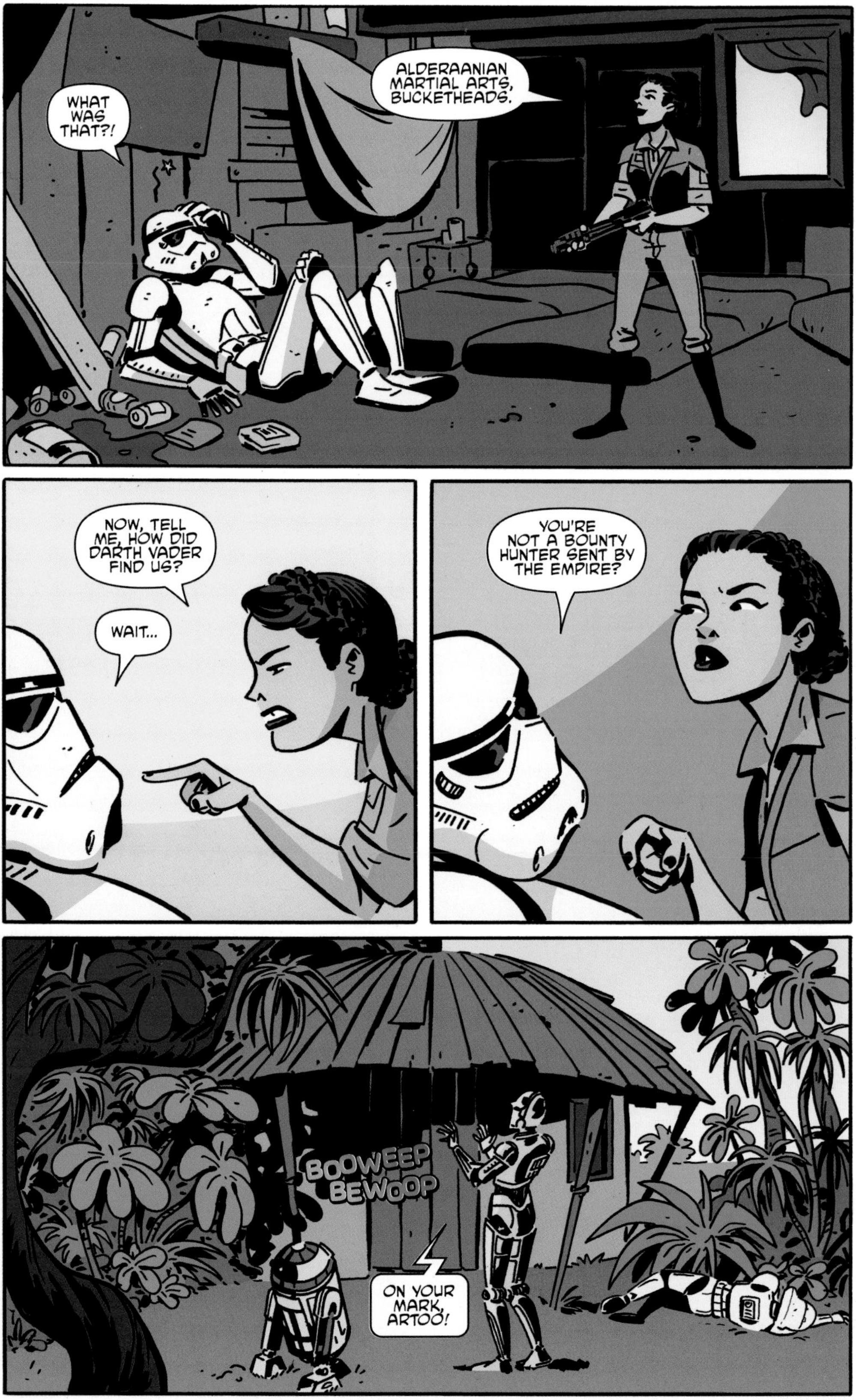
WHAT WAS THAT?!
ALDERAANIAN MARTIAL ARTS, BUCKETHEADS.
NOW, TELL ME, HOW DID DARTH VADER FIND US?
WAIT...
YOU'RE NOT A BOUNTY HUNTER SENT BY THE EMPIRE?
BOOWEEP BEWOOP
ON YOUR MARK, ARTOO!

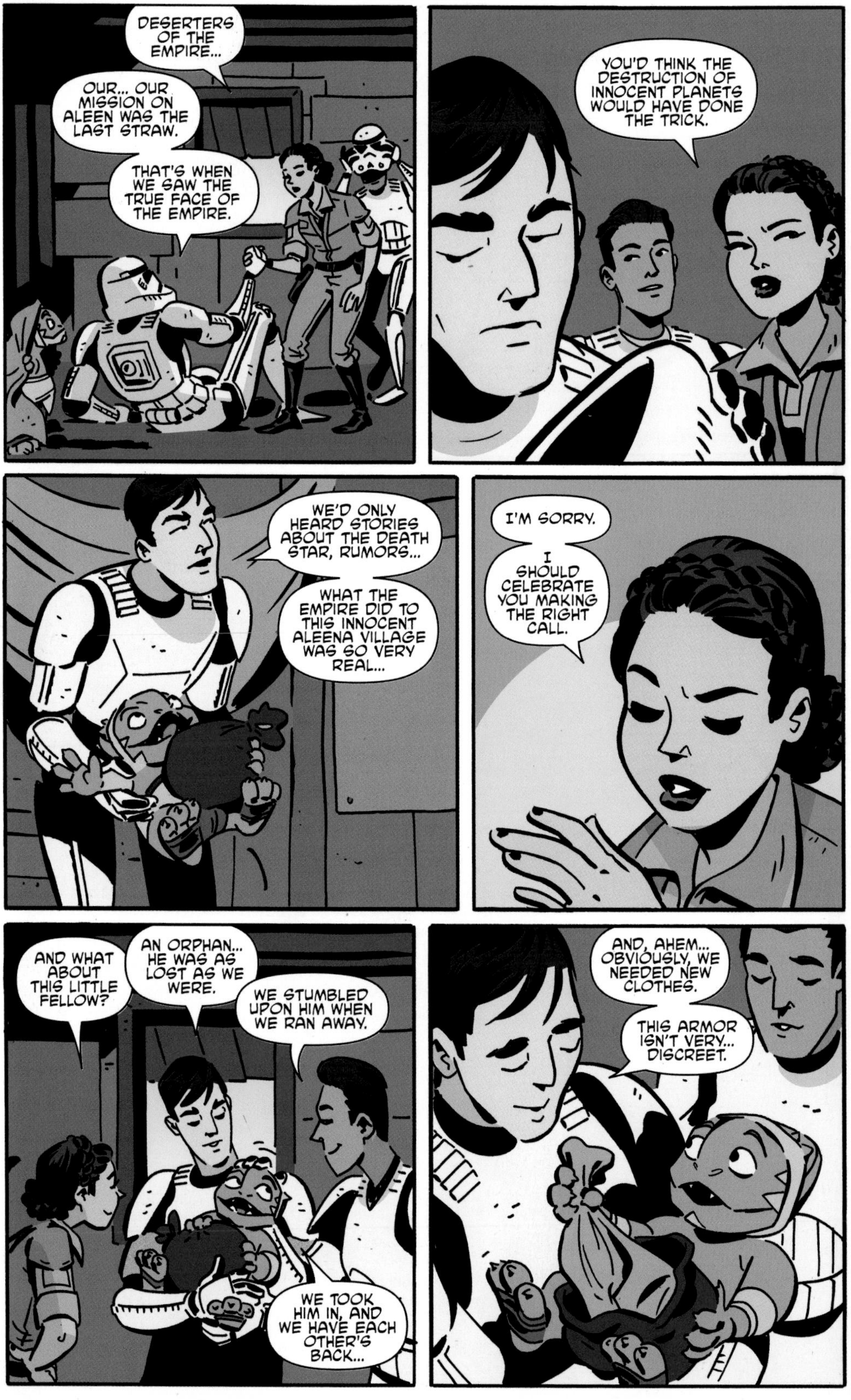
DESERTERS OF THE EMPIRE...
OUR... OUR MISSION ON ALEEN WAS THE LAST STRAW.
THAT'S WHEN WE SAW THE TRUE FACE OF THE EMPIRE.
YOU'D THINK THE DESTRUCTION OF INNOCENT PLANETS WOULD HAVE DONE THE TRICK.
WE'D ONLY HEARD STORIES ABOUT THE DEATH STAR, RUMORS...
WHAT THE EMPIRE DID TO THIS INNOCENT ALEENA VILLAGE WAS SO VERY REAL...
I'M SORRY.
I SHOULD CELEBRATE YOU MAKING THE RIGHT CALL.
AND WHAT ABOUT THIS LITTLE FELLOW?
AN ORPHAN... HE WAS AS LOST AS WE WERE.
WE STUMBLED UPON HIM WHEN WE RAN AWAY.
WE TOOK HIM IN, AND WE HAVE EACH OTHER'S BACK...
AND, AHEM... OBVIOUSLY, WE NEEDED NEW CLOTHES.
THIS ARMOR ISN'T VERY... DISCREET.

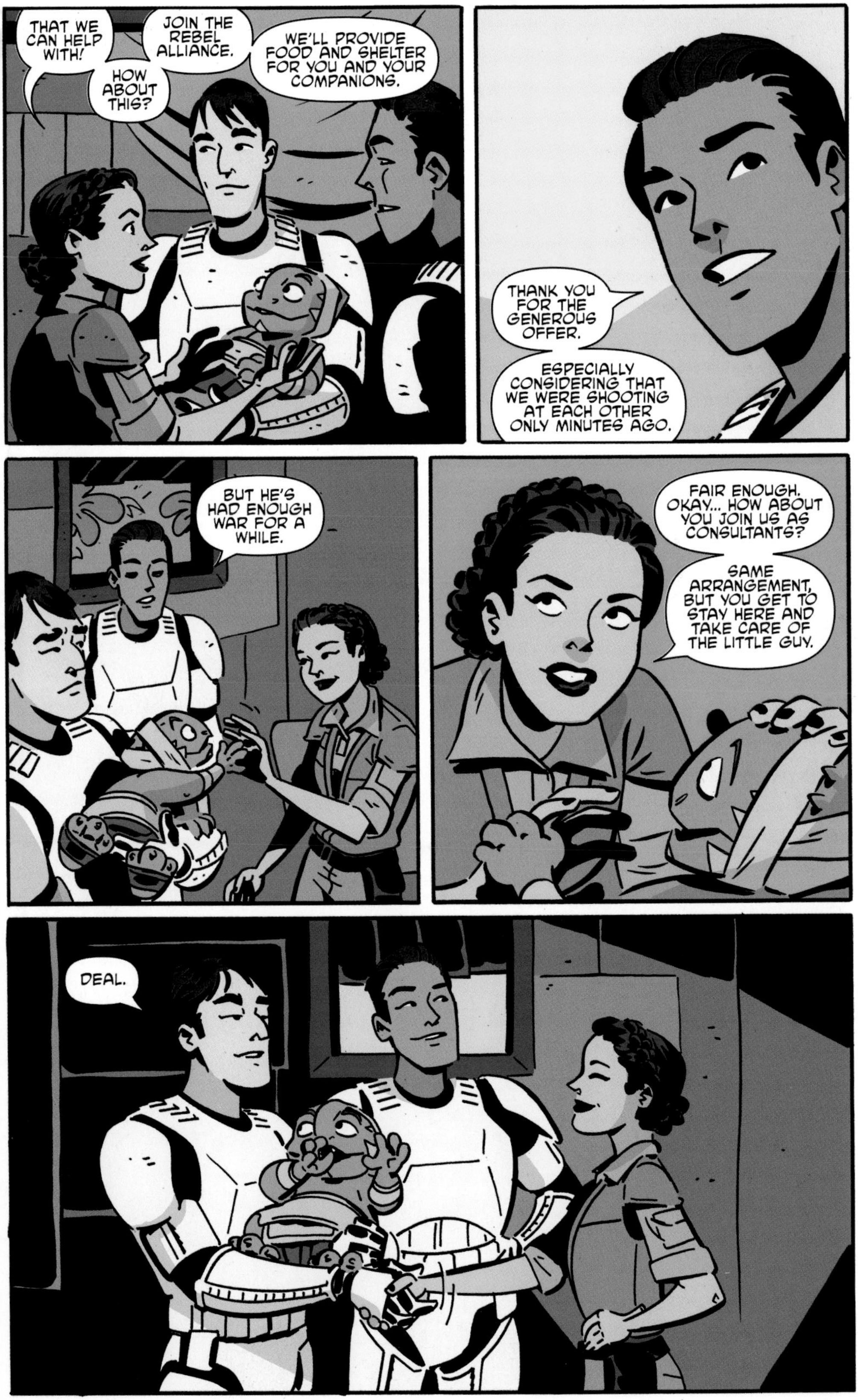
THAT WE CAN HELP WITH!
HOW ABOUT THIS?
JOIN THE REBEL ALLIANCE.
WE'LL PROVIDE FOOD AND SHELTER FOR YOU AND YOUR COMPANIONS.
THANK YOU FOR THE GENEROUS OFFER.
ESPECIALLY CONSIDERING THAT WE WERE SHOOTING AT EACH OTHER ONLY MINUTES AGO.
BUT HE'S HAD ENOUGH WAR FOR A WHILE.
FAIR ENOUGH. OKAY... HOW ABOUT YOU JOIN US AS CONSULTANTS?
SAME ARRANGEMENT, BUT YOU GET TO STAY HERE AND TAKE CARE OF THE LITTLE GUY.
DEAL.

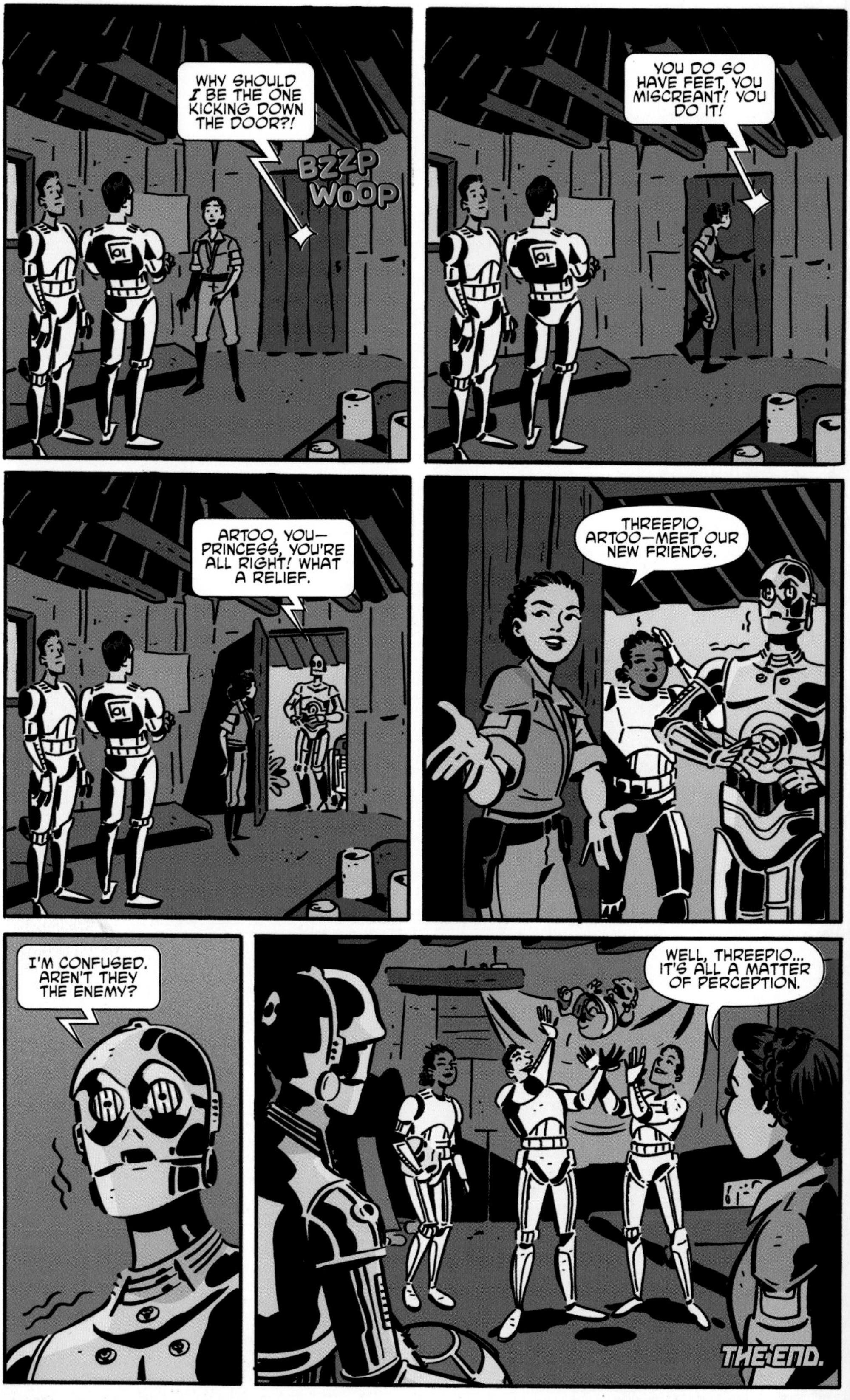
WHY SHOULD *I* BE THE ONE KICKING DOWN THE DOOR?!
BZZP WOOP
YOU DO SO HAVE FEET, YOU MISCREANT! YOU DO IT!
ARTOO, YOU— PRINCESS, YOU'RE ALL RIGHT! WHAT A RELIEF.
THREEPIO, ARTOO—MEET OUR NEW FRIENDS.
I'M CONFUSED. AREN'T THEY THE ENEMY?
WELL, THREEPIO... IT'S ALL A MATTER OF PERCEPTION.
THE END.

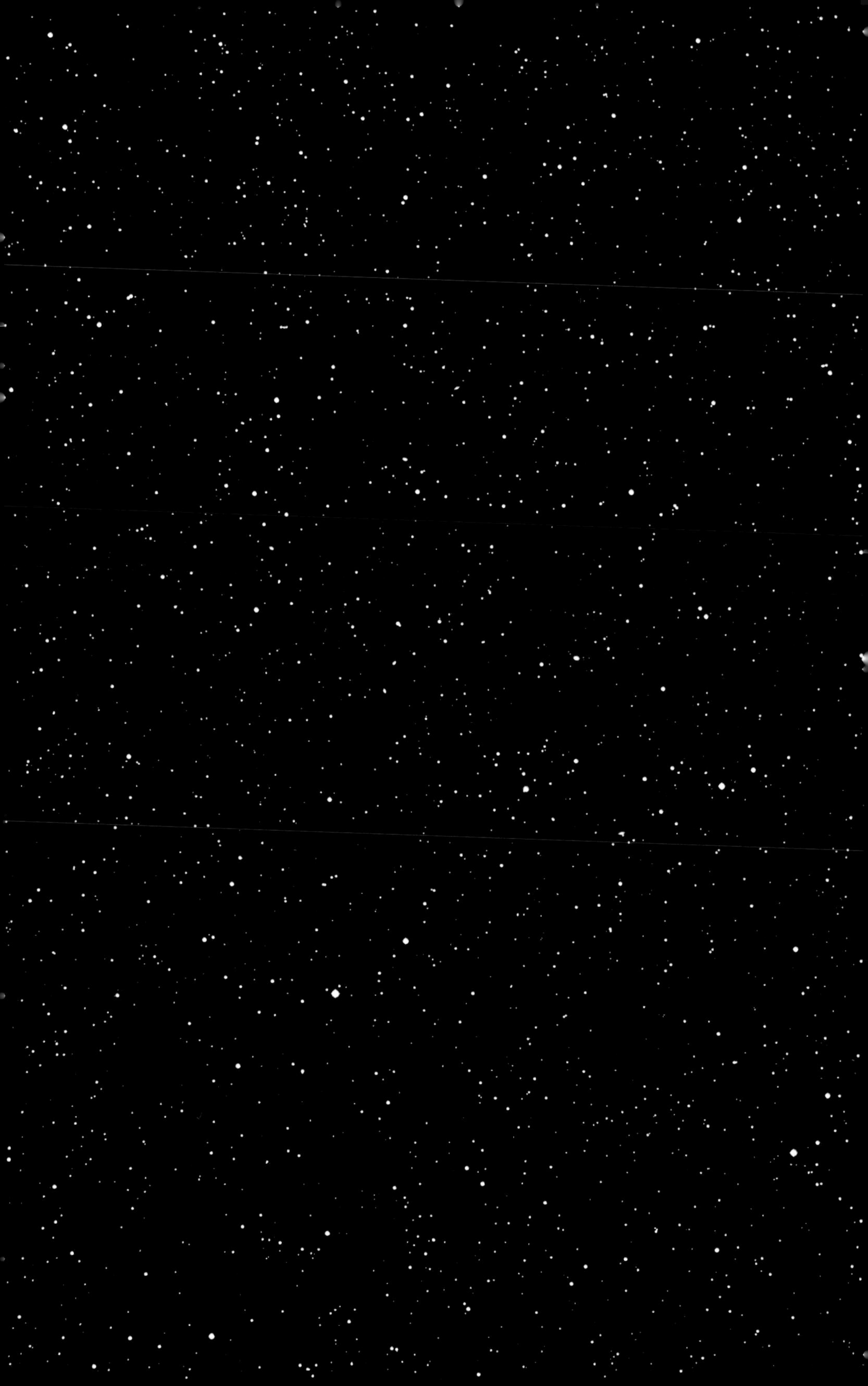

STAR WARS
ADVENTURES

A Race for Answers

WRITER
IAN FLYNN

ARTIST
TONY FLEECS

COLOR FLATTER
LAUREN PERRY

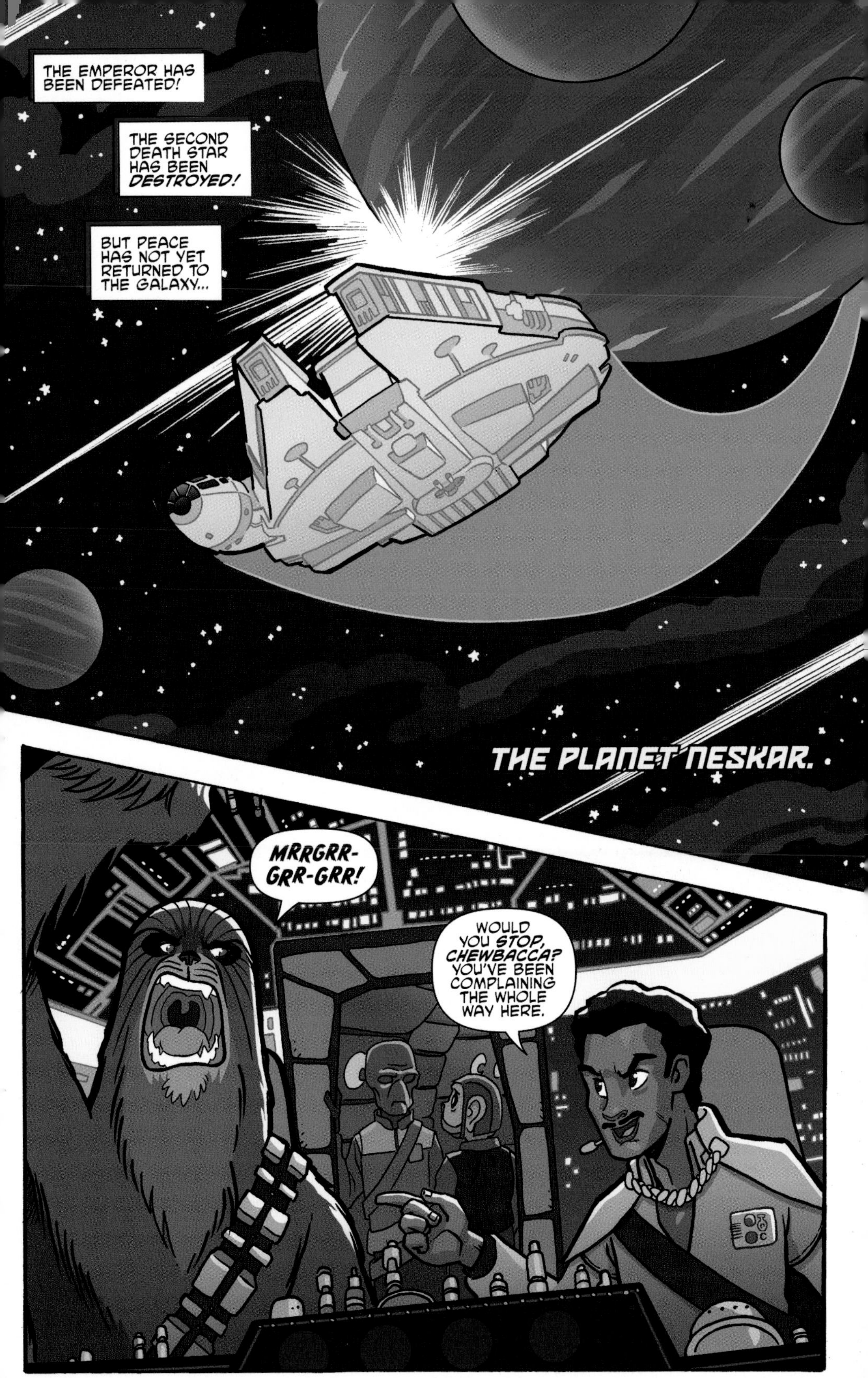
THE EMPEROR HAS BEEN DEFEATED!
THE SECOND DEATH STAR HAS BEEN *DESTROYED!*
BUT PEACE HAS NOT YET RETURNED TO THE GALAXY...
THE PLANET NESKAR.
MRRGRR-GRR-GRR!
WOULD YOU *STOP, CHEWBACCA?* YOU'VE BEEN COMPLAINING THE WHOLE WAY HERE.

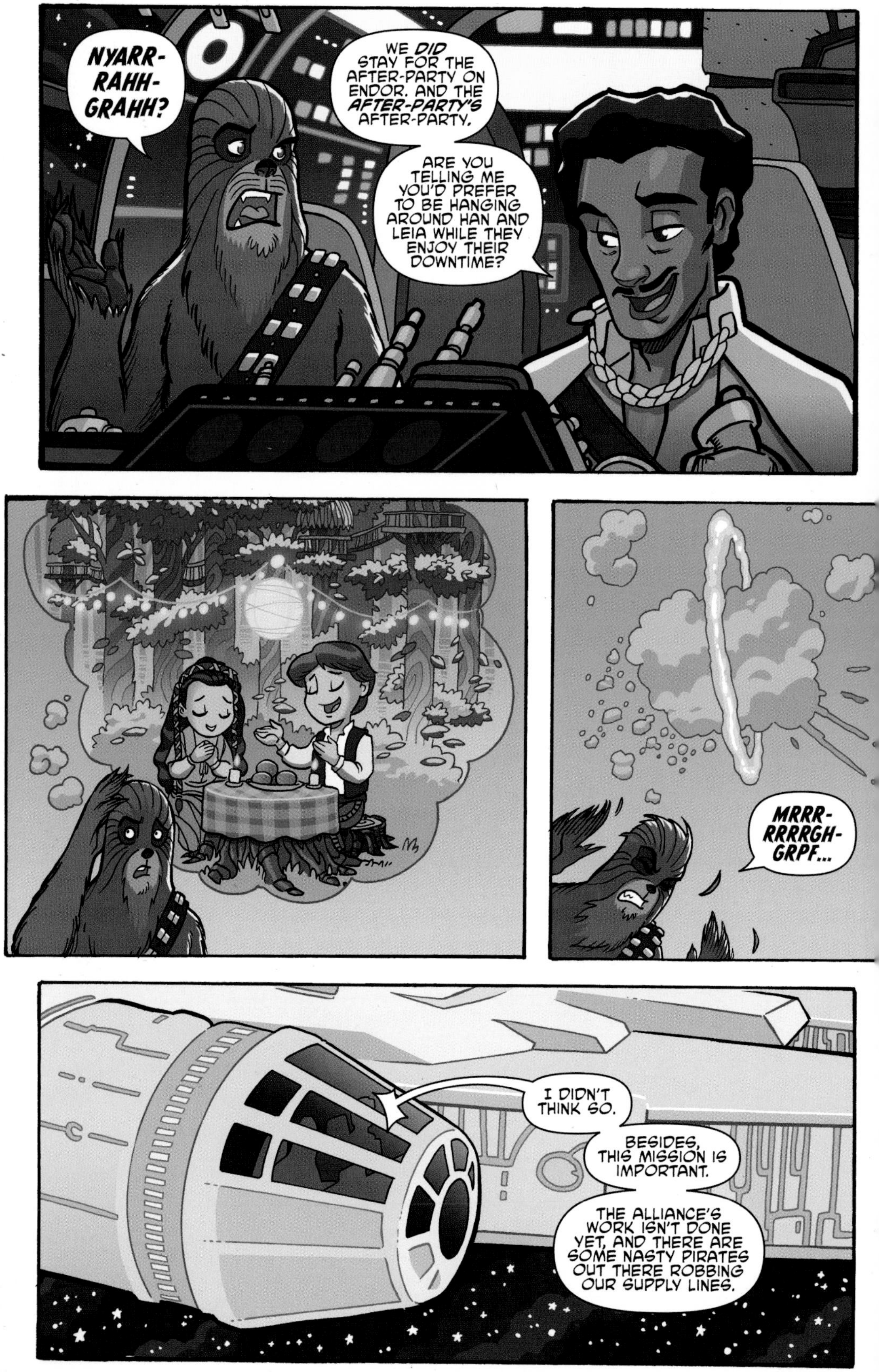
NYARR-RAHH-GRAHH?
WE *DID* STAY FOR THE AFTER-PARTY ON ENDOR. AND THE *AFTER-PARTY'S* AFTER-PARTY.
ARE YOU TELLING ME YOU'D PREFER TO BE HANGING AROUND HAN AND LEIA WHILE THEY ENJOY THEIR DOWNTIME?
MRRR-RRRRGH-GRPF...
I DIDN'T THINK SO.
BESIDES, THIS MISSION IS IMPORTANT.
THE ALLIANCE'S WORK ISN'T DONE YET, AND THERE ARE SOME NASTY PIRATES OUT THERE ROBBING OUR SUPPLY LINES.

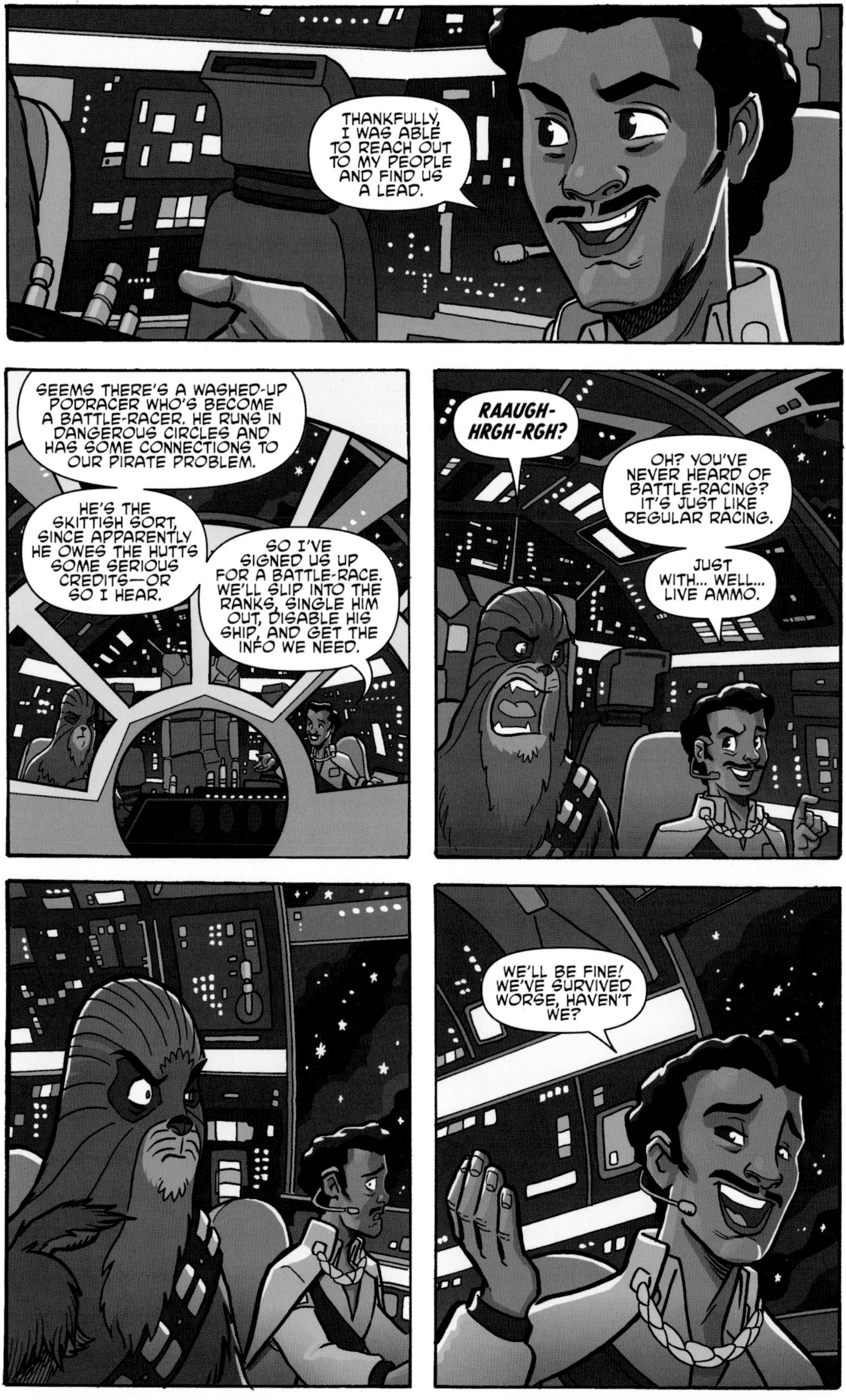
THANKFULLY, I WAS ABLE TO REACH OUT TO MY PEOPLE AND FIND US A LEAD.
SEEMS THERE'S A WASHED-UP PODRACER WHO'S BECOME A BATTLE-RACER. HE RUNS IN DANGEROUS CIRCLES AND HAS SOME CONNECTIONS TO OUR PIRATE PROBLEM.
HE'S THE SKITTISH SORT, SINCE APPARENTLY HE OWES THE HUTTS SOME SERIOUS CREDITS—OR SO I HEAR.
SO I'VE SIGNED US UP FOR A BATTLE-RACE. WE'LL SLIP INTO THE RANKS, SINGLE HIM OUT, DISABLE HIS SHIP, AND GET THE INFO WE NEED.
RAAUGH-HRGH-RGH?
OH? YOU'VE NEVER HEARD OF BATTLE-RACING? IT'S JUST LIKE REGULAR RACING.
JUST WITH... WELL... LIVE AMMO.
WE'LL BE FINE! WE'VE SURVIVED WORSE, HAVEN'T WE?

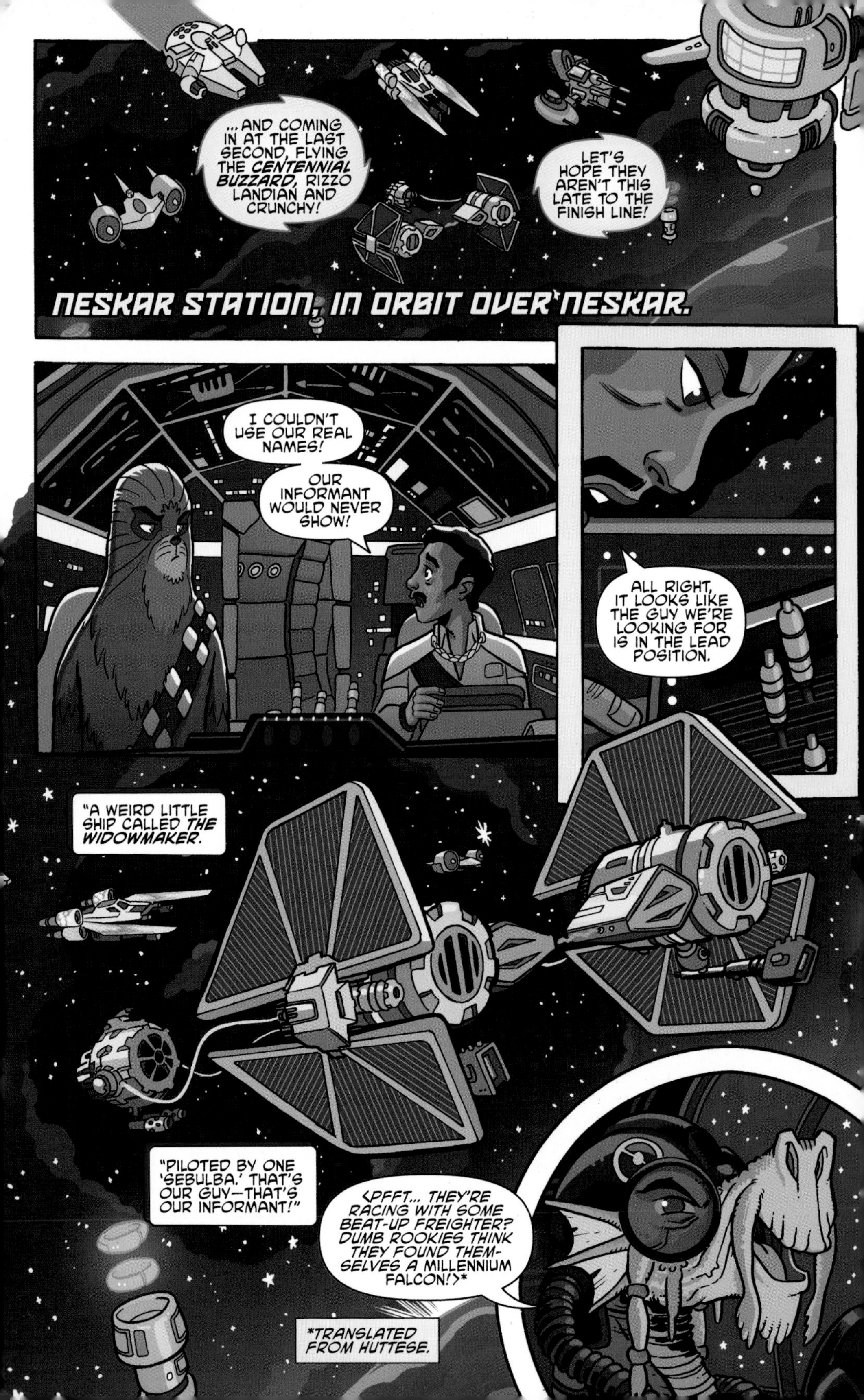

...AND COMING IN AT THE LAST SECOND, FLYING THE CENTENNIAL BUZZARD, RIZZO LANDIAN AND CRUNCHY!
LET'S HOPE THEY AREN'T THIS LATE TO THE FINISH LINE!
NESKAR STATION, IN ORBIT OVER NESKAR.
I COULDN'T USE OUR REAL NAMES!
OUR INFORMANT WOULD NEVER SHOW!
ALL RIGHT, IT LOOKS LIKE THE GUY WE'RE LOOKING FOR IS IN THE LEAD POSITION.
"A WEIRD LITTLE SHIP CALLED THE WIDOWMAKER.
"PILOTED BY ONE 'SEBULBA.' THAT'S OUR GUY—THAT'S OUR INFORMANT!"
<PFFT... THEY'RE RACING WITH SOME BEAT-UP FREIGHTER? DUMB ROOKIES THINK THEY FOUND THEMSELVES A MILLENNIUM FALCON!>*
*TRANSLATED FROM HUTTESE.

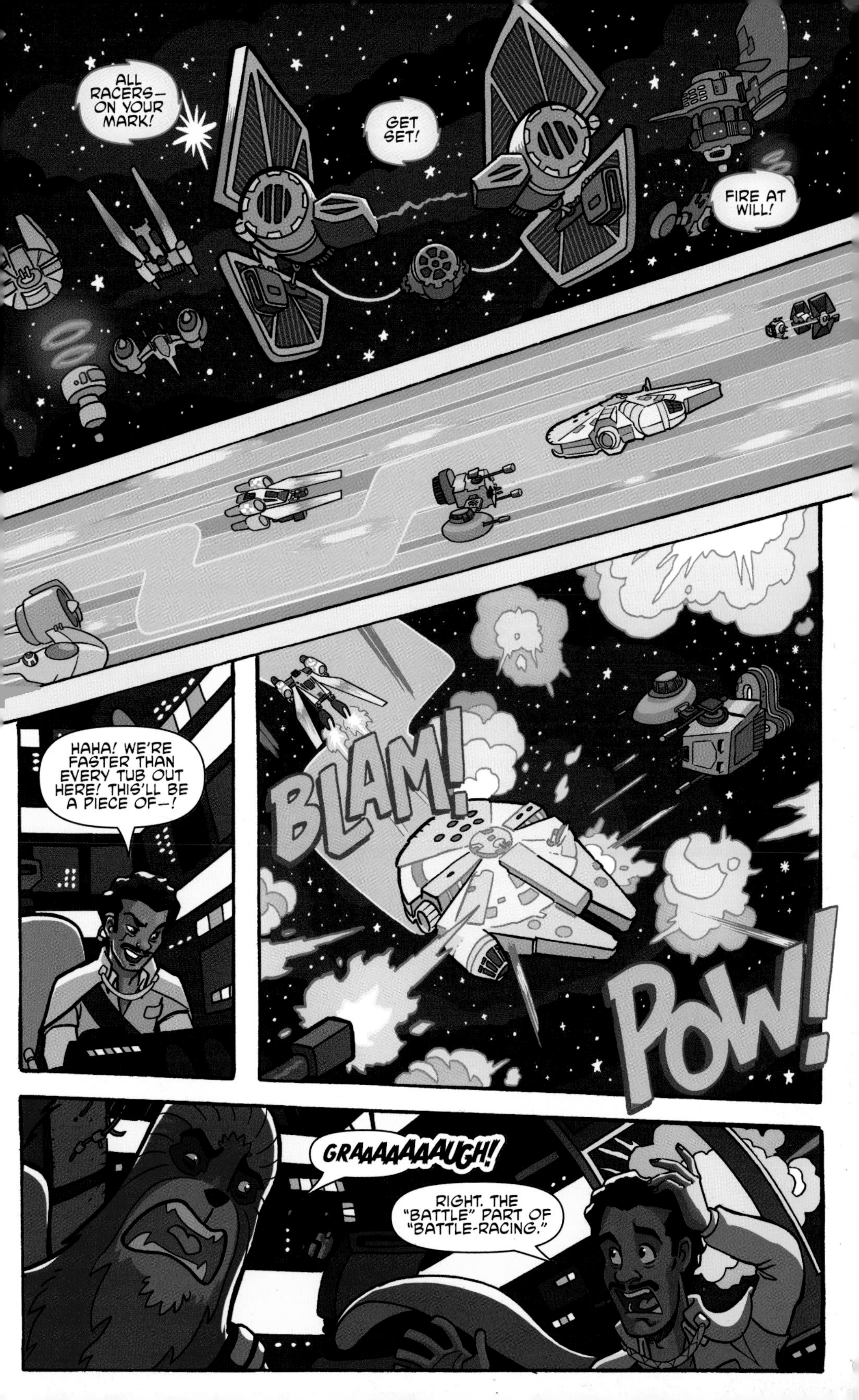
ALL RACERS— ON YOUR MARK!
GET SET!
FIRE AT WILL!
HAHA! WE'RE FASTER THAN EVERY TUB OUT HERE! THIS'LL BE A PIECE OF—!
BLAM!
POW!
GRAAAAAAAUGH!
RIGHT. THE "BATTLE" PART OF "BATTLE-RACING."

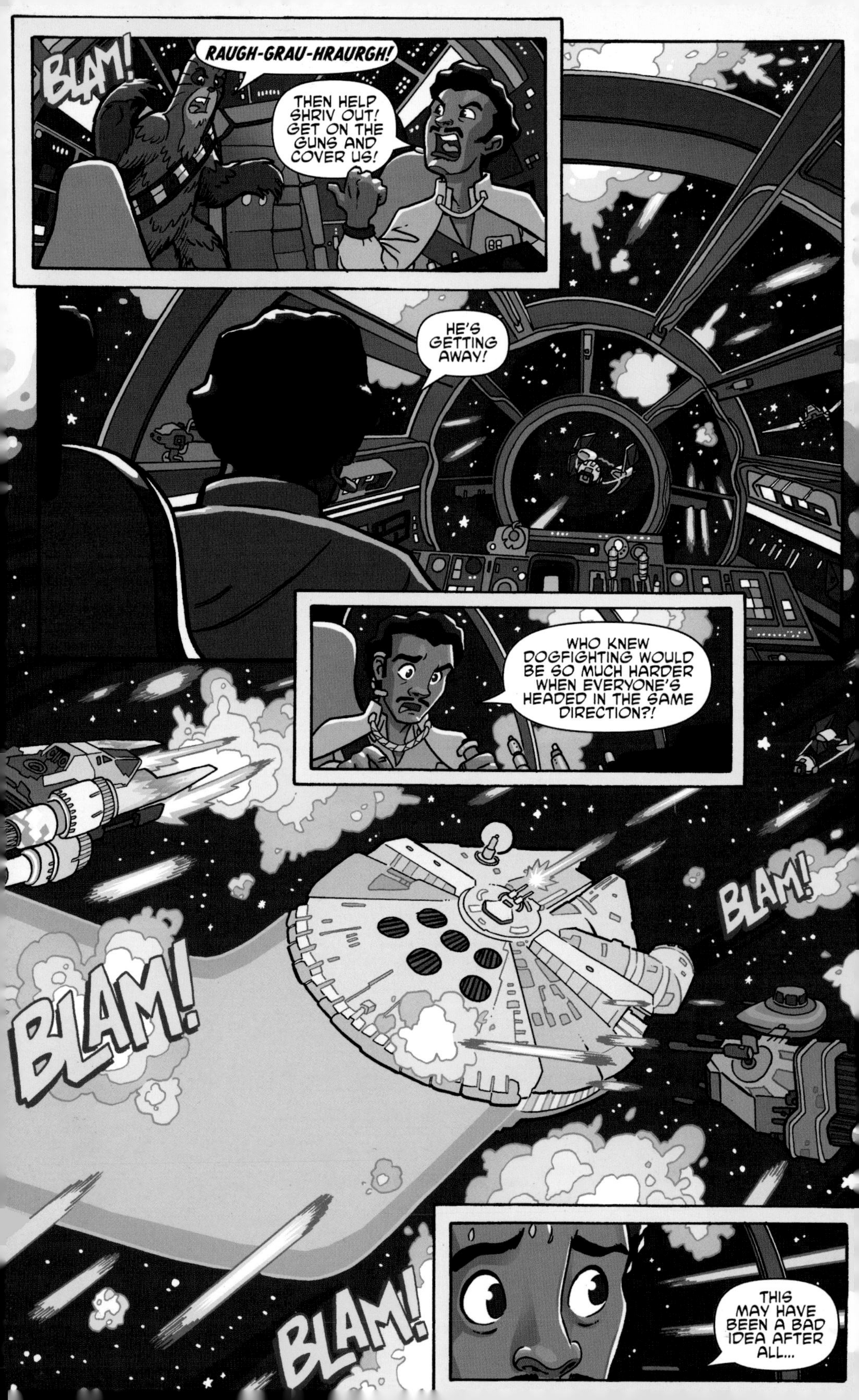
BLAM!
RAUGH-GRAU-HRAURGH!
THEN HELP SHRIV OUT! GET ON THE GUNS AND COVER US!
HE'S GETTING AWAY!
WHO KNEW DOGFIGHTING WOULD BE SO MUCH HARDER WHEN EVERYONE'S HEADED IN THE SAME DIRECTION?!
BLAM!
BLAM!
BLAM!
THIS MAY HAVE BEEN A BAD IDEA AFTER ALL...

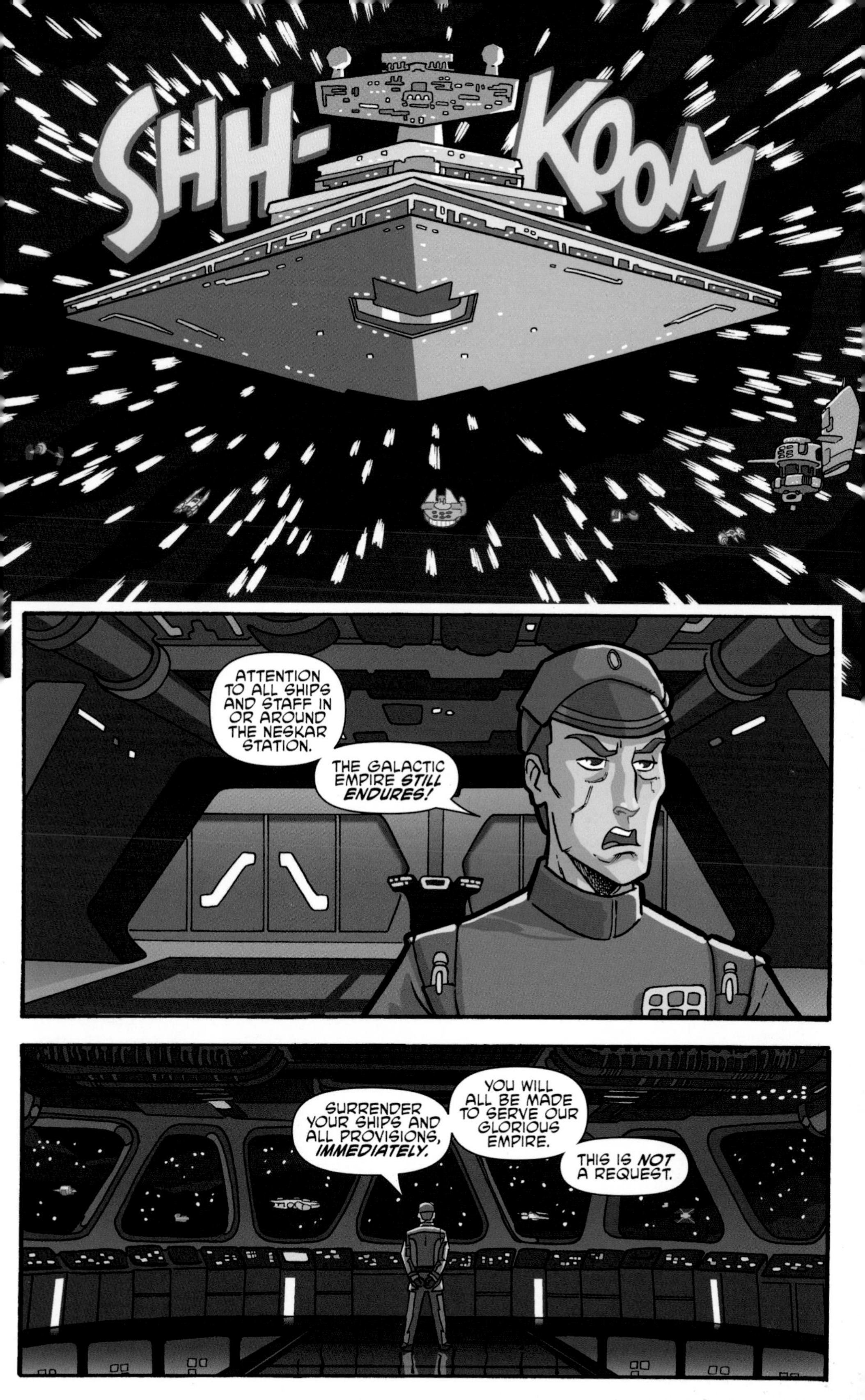
SHH-KOOM
ATTENTION TO ALL SHIPS AND STAFF IN OR AROUND THE NESKAR STATION.
THE GALACTIC EMPIRE *STILL ENDURES!*
SURRENDER YOUR SHIPS AND ALL PROVISIONS, *IMMEDIATELY.*
YOU WILL ALL BE MADE TO SERVE OUR GLORIOUS EMPIRE.
THIS IS *NOT* A REQUEST.

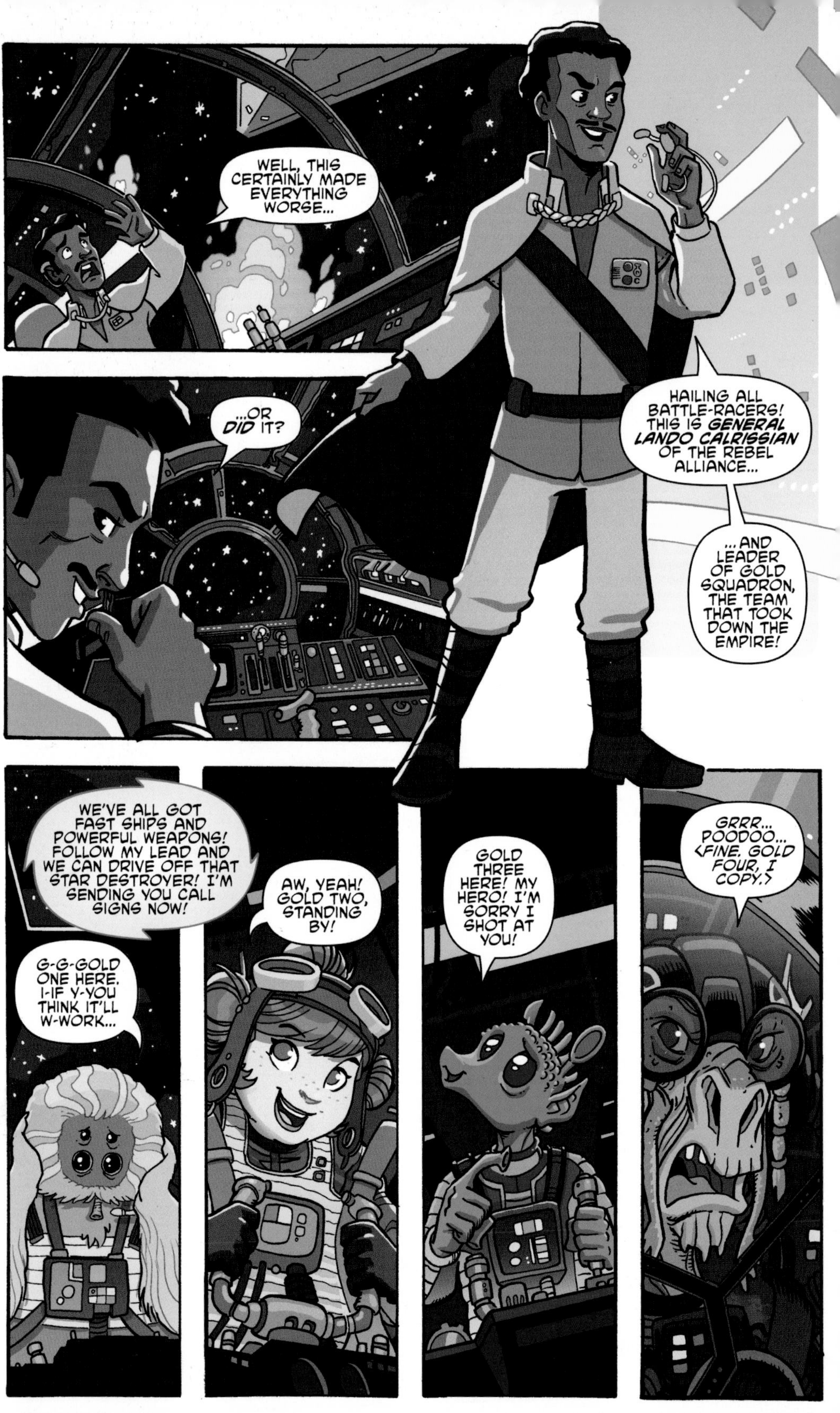
WELL, THIS CERTAINLY MADE EVERYTHING WORSE...
...OR DID IT?
HAILING ALL BATTLE-RACERS! THIS IS GENERAL LANDO CALRISSIAN OF THE REBEL ALLIANCE...
...AND LEADER OF GOLD SQUADRON, THE TEAM THAT TOOK DOWN THE EMPIRE!
WE'VE ALL GOT FAST SHIPS AND POWERFUL WEAPONS! FOLLOW MY LEAD AND WE CAN DRIVE OFF THAT STAR DESTROYER! I'M SENDING YOU CALL SIGNS NOW!
G-G-GOLD ONE HERE. I-IF Y-YOU THINK IT'LL W-WORK...
AW, YEAH! GOLD TWO, STANDING BY!
GOLD THREE HERE! MY HERO! I'M SORRY I SHOT AT YOU!
GRRR... POODOO... <FINE. GOLD FOUR, I COPY.>

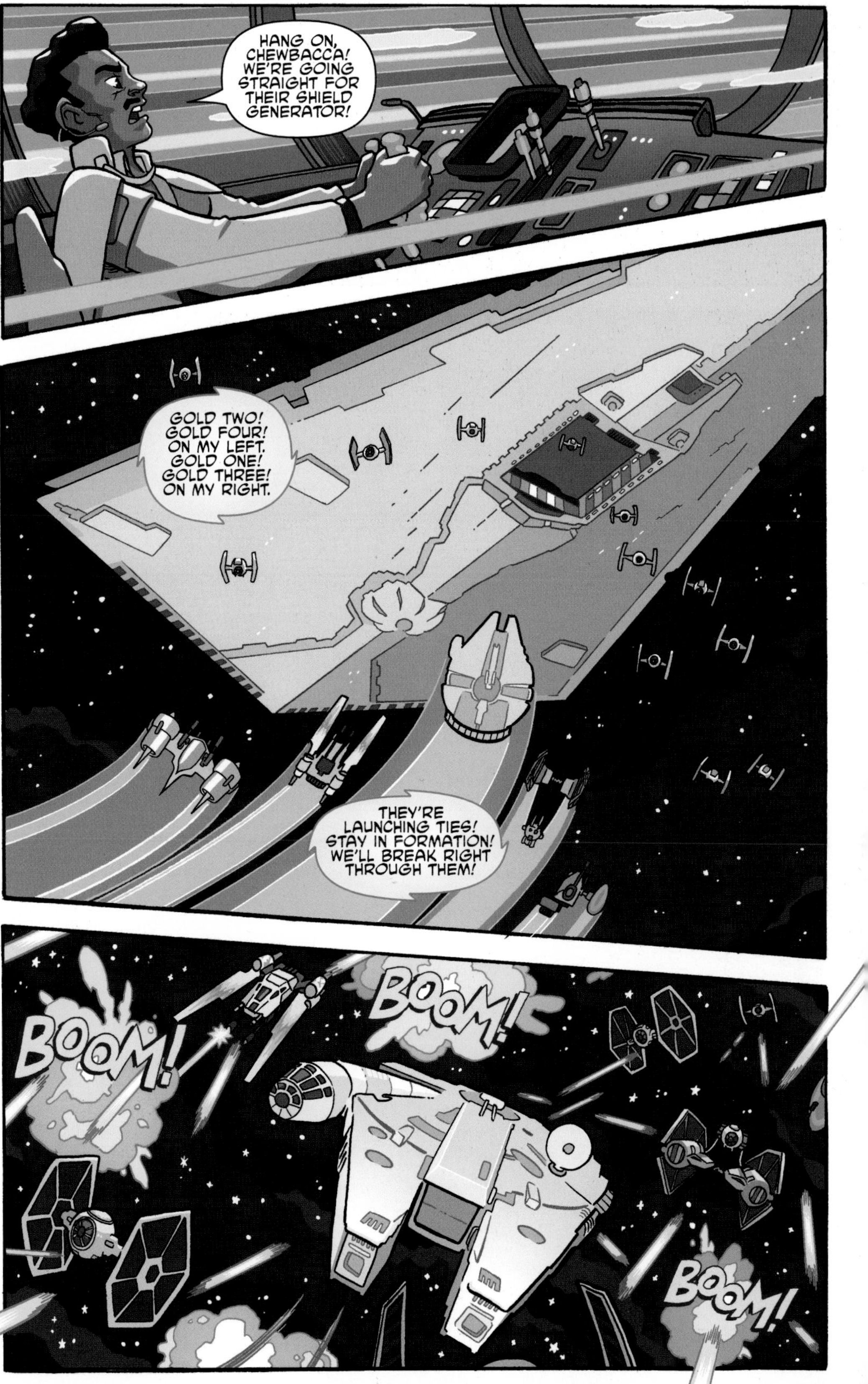
HANG ON, CHEWBACCA! WE'RE GOING STRAIGHT FOR THEIR SHIELD GENERATOR!
GOLD TWO! GOLD FOUR! ON MY LEFT. GOLD ONE! GOLD THREE! ON MY RIGHT.
THEY'RE LAUNCHING TIES! STAY IN FORMATION! WE'LL BREAK RIGHT THROUGH THEM!
BOOM!
BOOM!
BOOM!

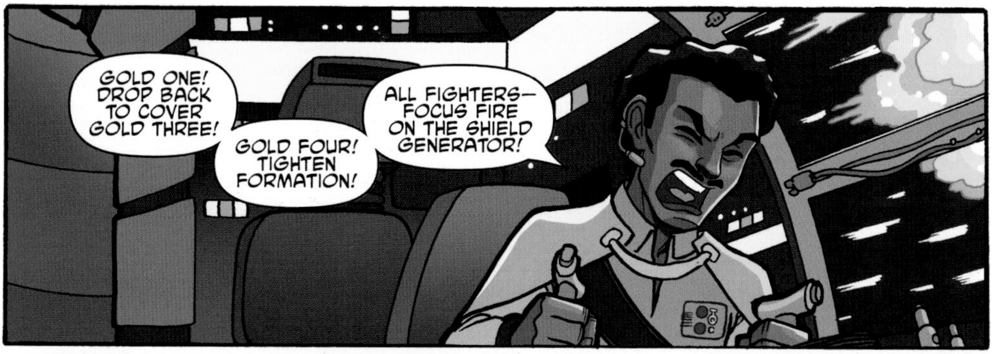
GOLD ONE! DROP BACK TO COVER GOLD THREE!
GOLD FOUR! TIGHTEN FORMATION!
ALL FIGHTERS— FOCUS FIRE ON THE SHIELD GENERATOR!

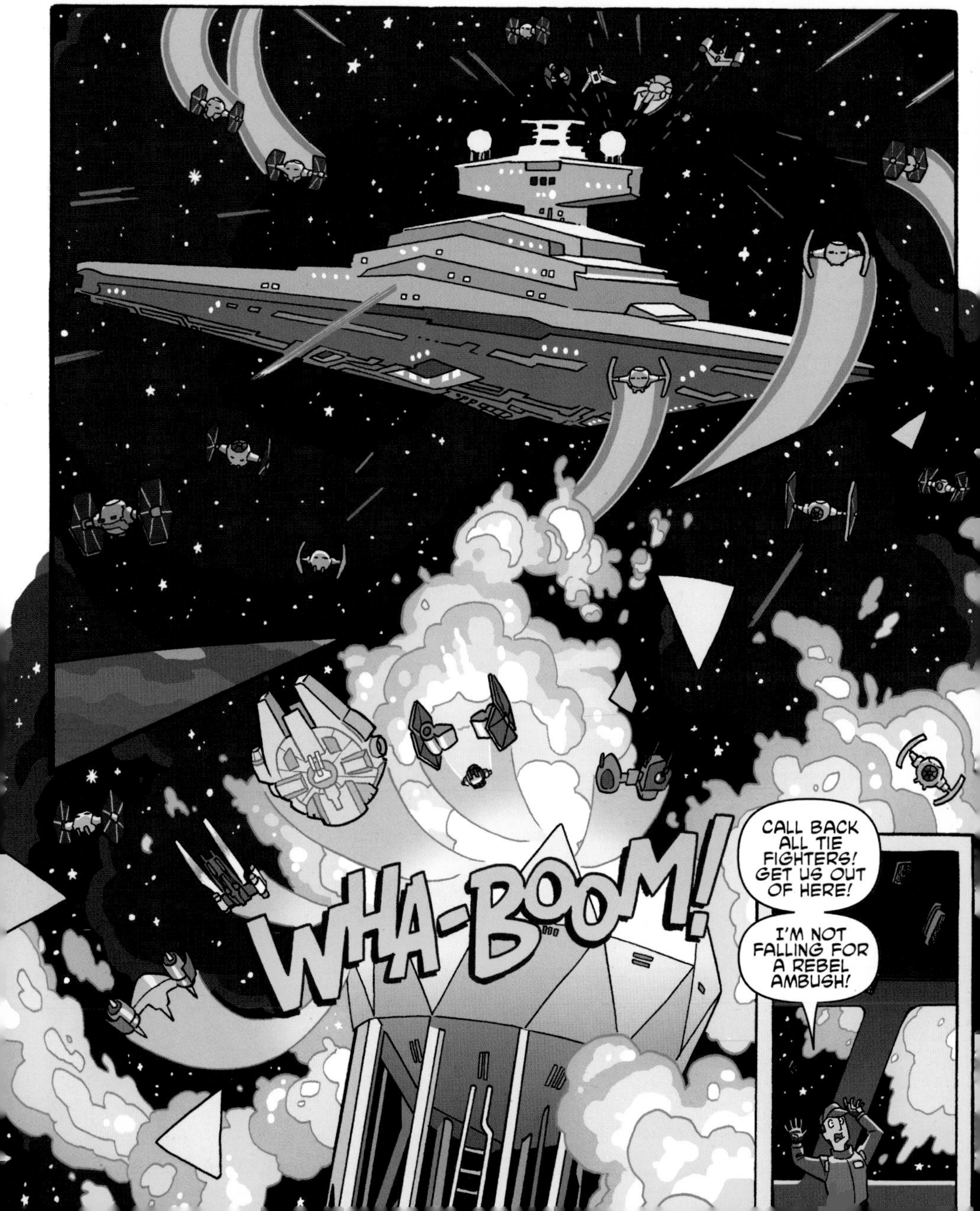
WHA-BOOM!
CALL BACK ALL TIE FIGHTERS! GET US OUT OF HERE!
I'M NOT FALLING FOR A REBEL AMBUSH!

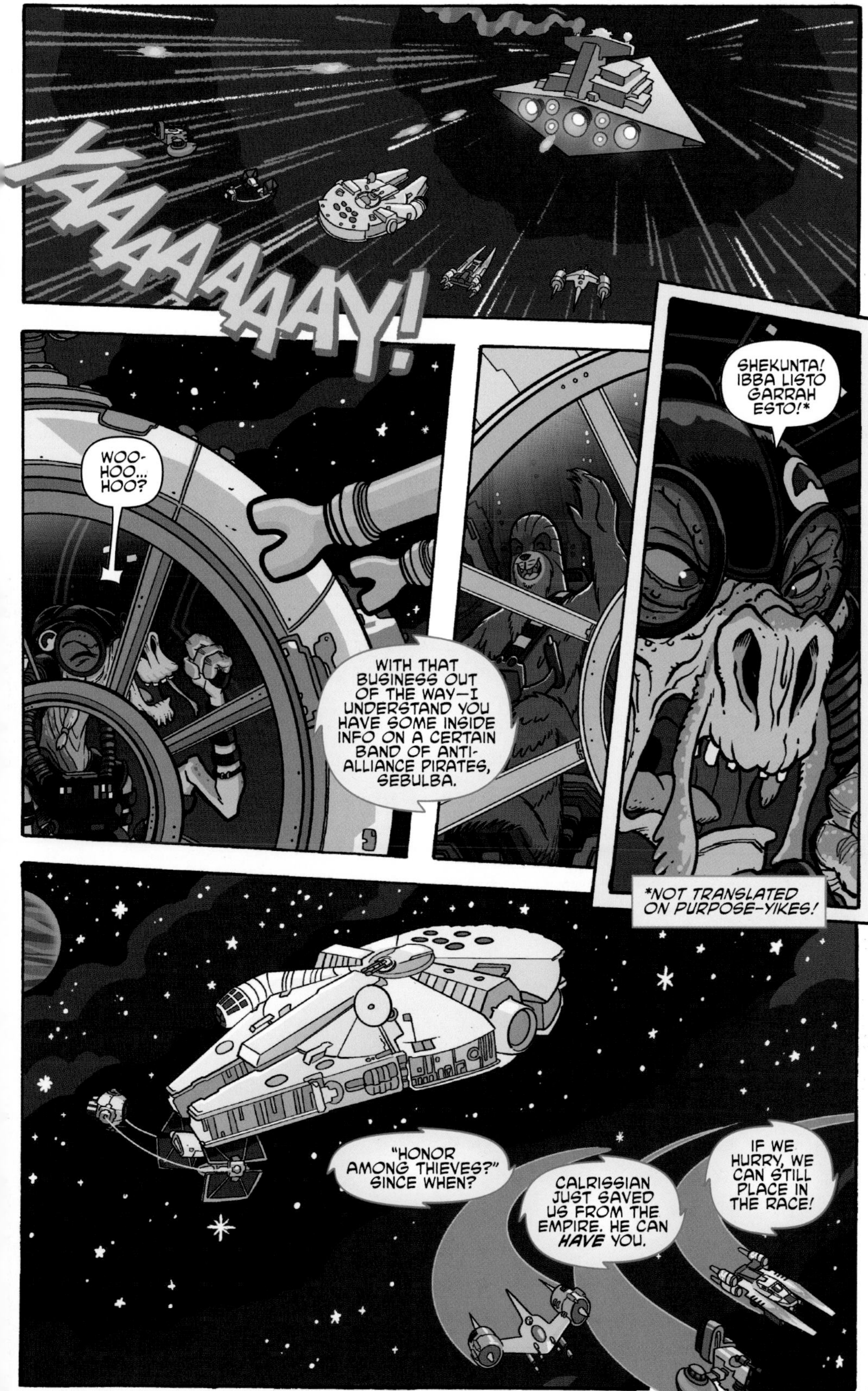
YAAAAAAAY!
WOO-HOO... HOO?
WITH THAT BUSINESS OUT OF THE WAY—I UNDERSTAND YOU HAVE SOME INSIDE INFO ON A CERTAIN BAND OF ANTI-ALLIANCE PIRATES, SEBULBA.
SHEKUNTA! IBBA LISTO GARRAH ESTO!*
*NOT TRANSLATED ON PURPOSE–YIKES!
"HONOR AMONG THIEVES?" SINCE WHEN?
CALRISSIAN JUST SAVED US FROM THE EMPIRE. HE CAN *HAVE* YOU.
IF WE HURRY, WE CAN STILL PLACE IN THE RACE!

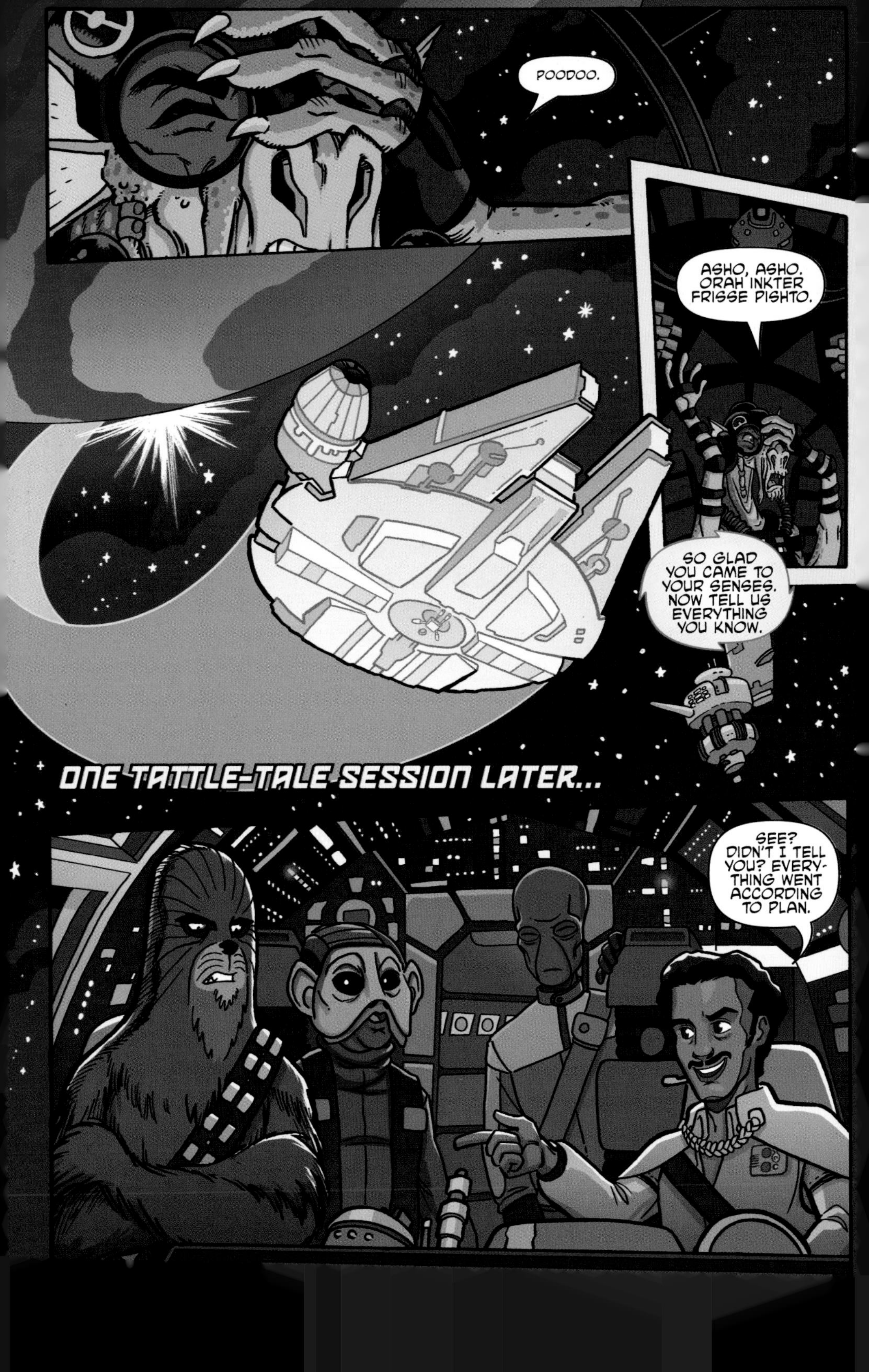
POODOO.
ASHO, ASHO. ORAH INKTER FRISSE PISHTO.
SO GLAD YOU CAME TO YOUR SENSES. NOW TELL US EVERYTHING YOU KNOW.
ONE TATTLE-TALE SESSION LATER...
SEE? DIDN'T I TELL YOU? EVERY-THING WENT ACCORDING TO PLAN.

TALES FROM WILD SPACE

The Heist

WRITER
SHANE MCCARTHY

ARTIST
NICOLETTA BALDARI

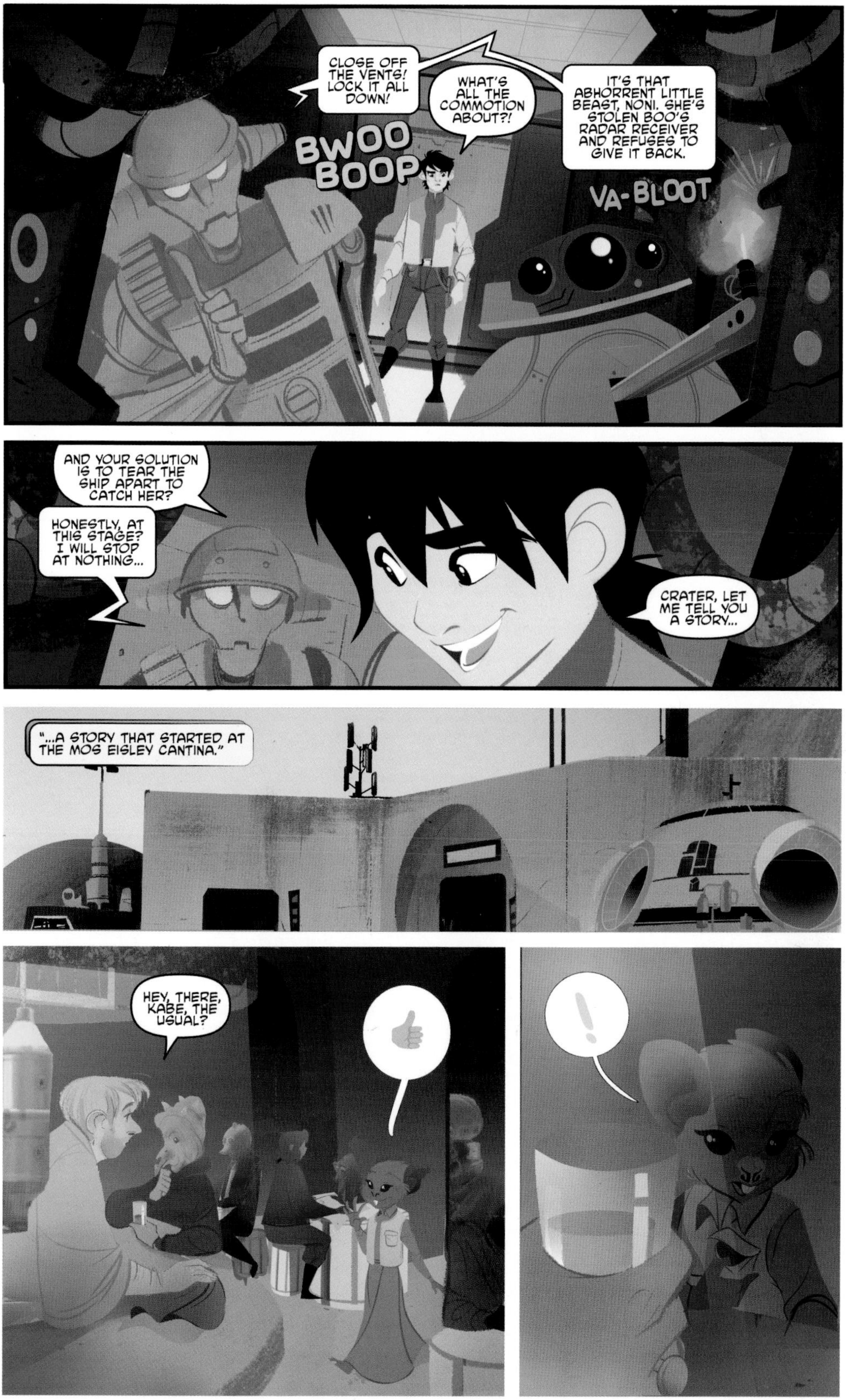
CLOSE OFF THE VENTS! LOCK IT ALL DOWN!
WHAT'S ALL THE COMMOTION ABOUT?!
IT'S THAT ABHORRENT LITTLE BEAST, NONI. SHE'S STOLEN BOO'S RADAR RECEIVER AND REFUSES TO GIVE IT BACK.
BWOO BOOP
VA-BLOOT
AND YOUR SOLUTION IS TO TEAR THE SHIP APART TO CATCH HER?
HONESTLY, AT THIS STAGE? I WILL STOP AT NOTHING...
CRATER, LET ME TELL YOU A STORY...
"...A STORY THAT STARTED AT THE MOS EISLEY CANTINA."
HEY, THERE, KABE, THE USUAL?
!

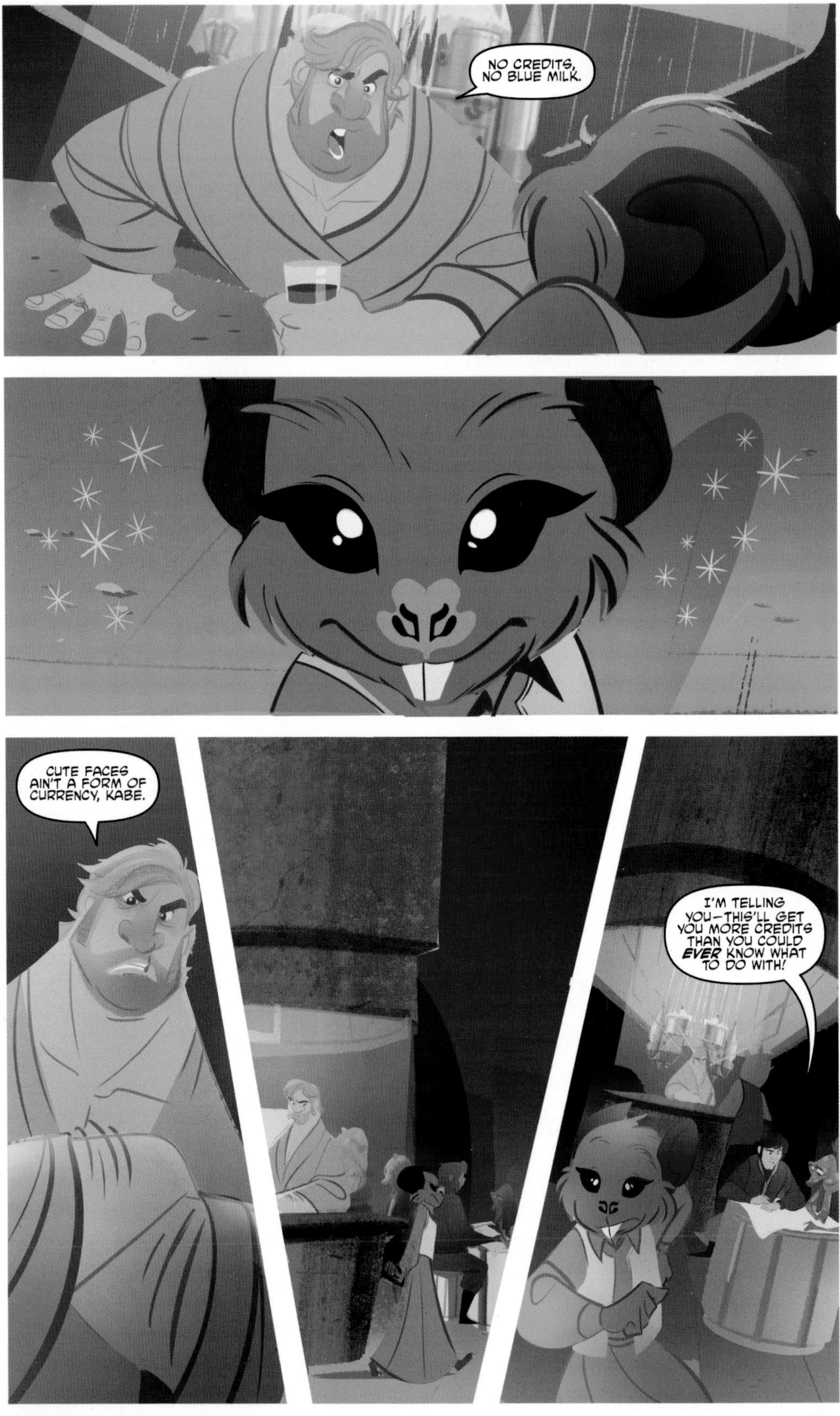
NO CREDITS, NO BLUE MILK.
CUTE FACES AIN'T A FORM OF CURRENCY, KABE.
I'M TELLING YOU—THIS'LL GET YOU MORE CREDITS THAN YOU COULD ***EVER*** KNOW WHAT TO DO WITH!

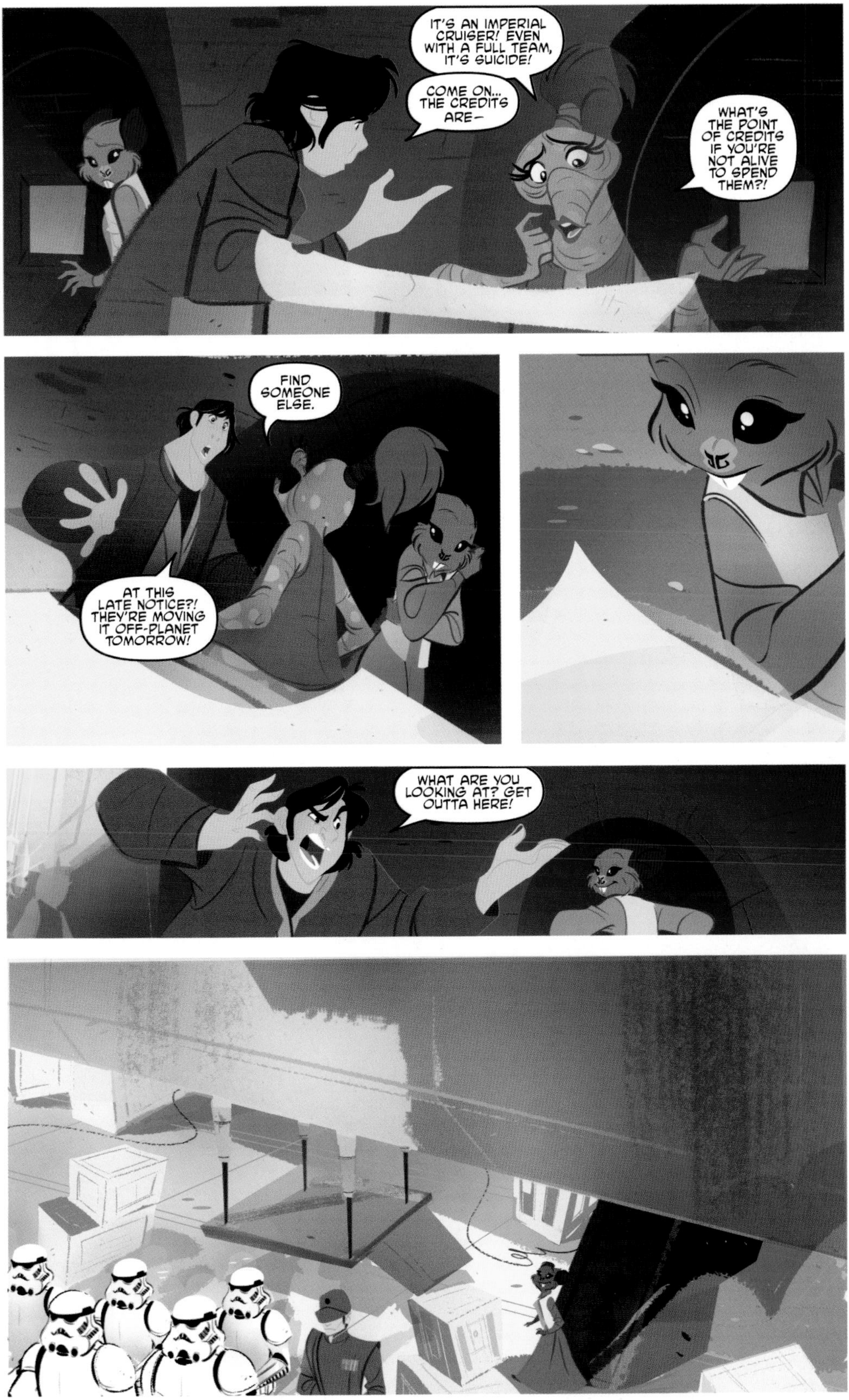
IT'S AN IMPERIAL CRUISER! EVEN WITH A FULL TEAM, IT'S SUICIDE!
COME ON... THE CREDITS ARE–
WHAT'S THE POINT OF CREDITS IF YOU'RE NOT ALIVE TO SPEND THEM?!
FIND SOMEONE ELSE.
AT THIS LATE NOTICE?! THEY'RE MOVING IT OFF-PLANET TOMORROW!
WHAT ARE YOU LOOKING AT? GET OUTTA HERE!

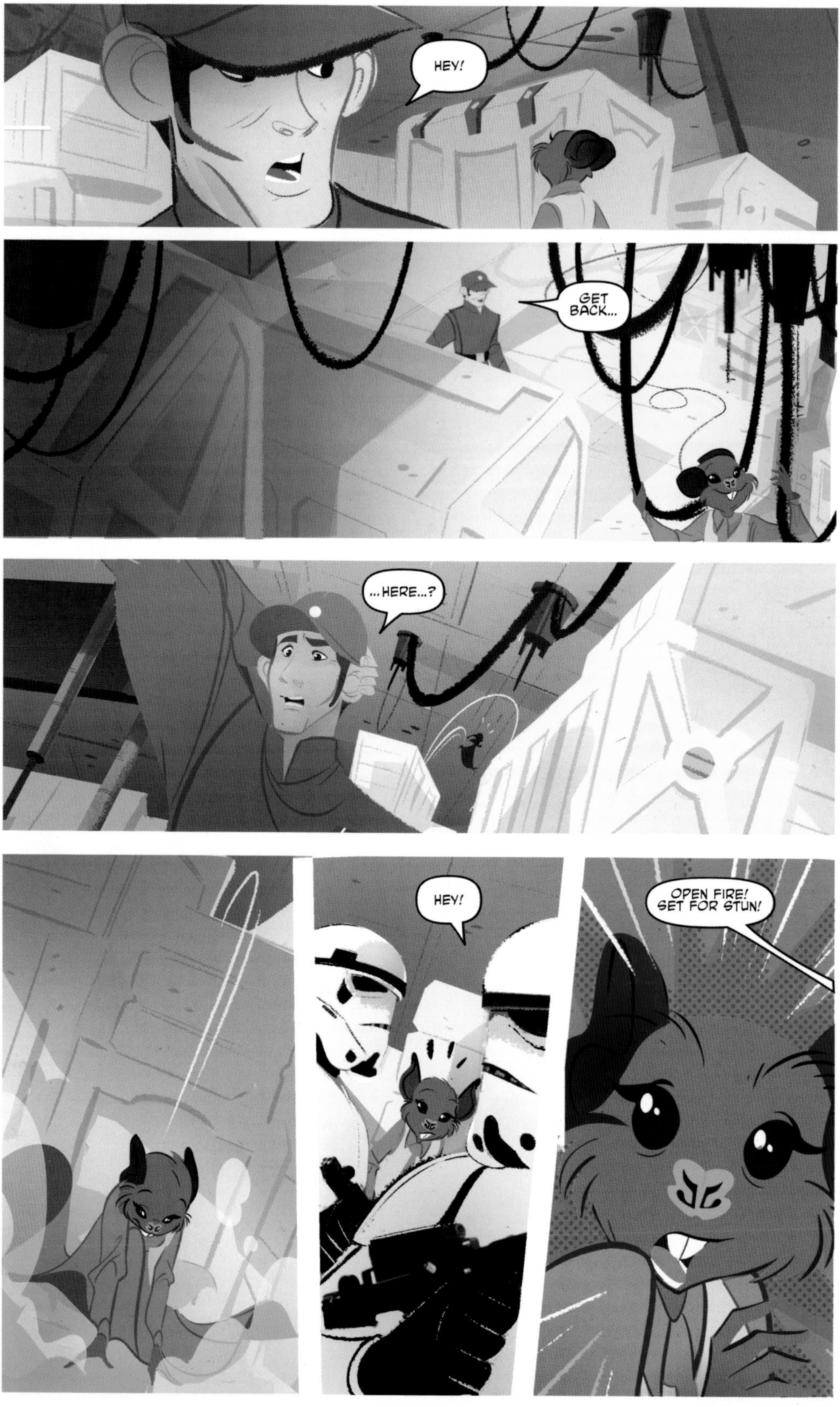
HEY!
GET BACK...
...HERE...?
HEY!
OPEN FIRE! SET FOR STUN!

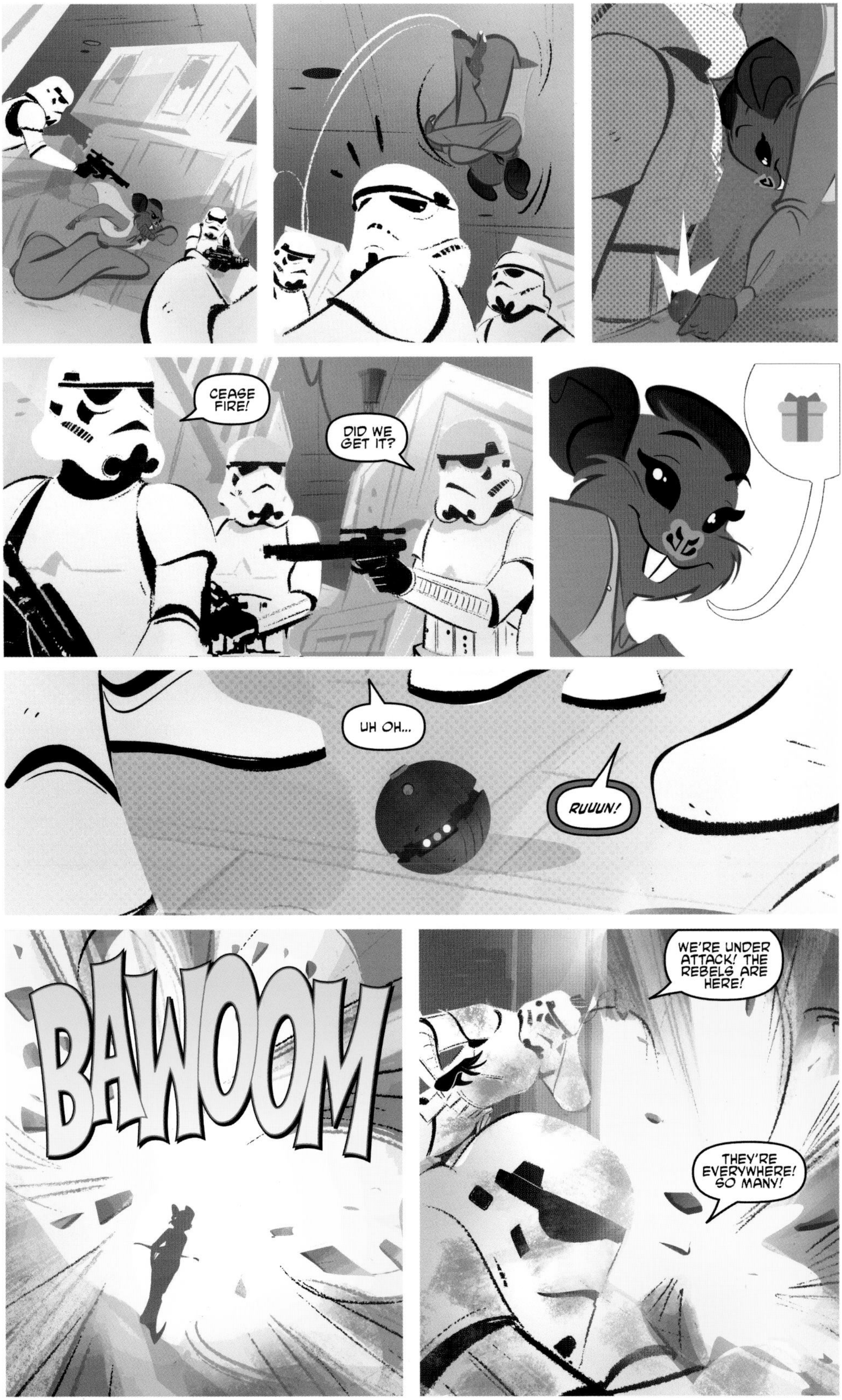

CEASE FIRE!
DID WE GET IT?
UH OH...
RUUUN!
BAWOOM
WE'RE UNDER ATTACK! THE REBELS ARE HERE!
THEY'RE EVERYWHERE! SO MANY!

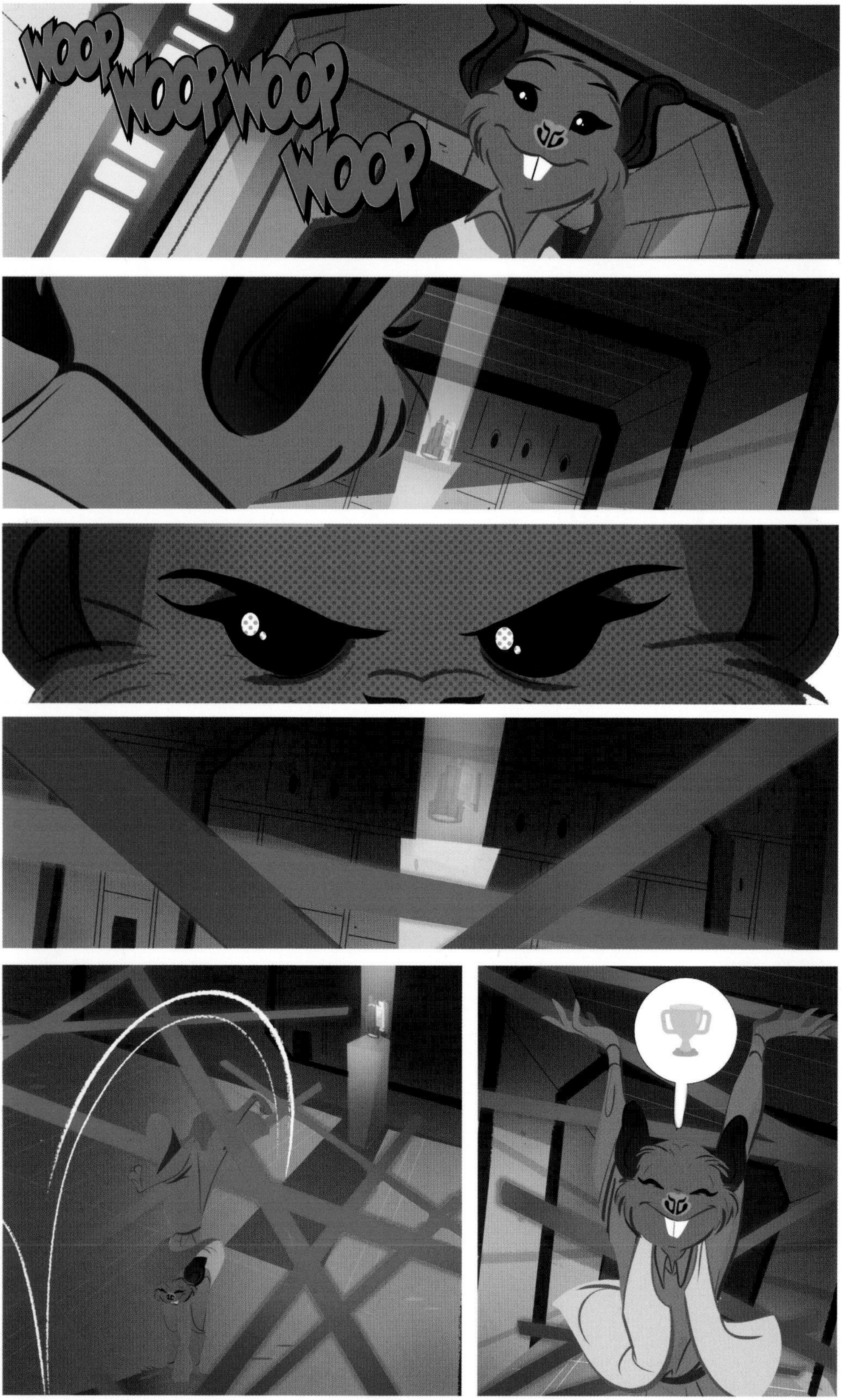
WOOP WOOP WOOP WOOP

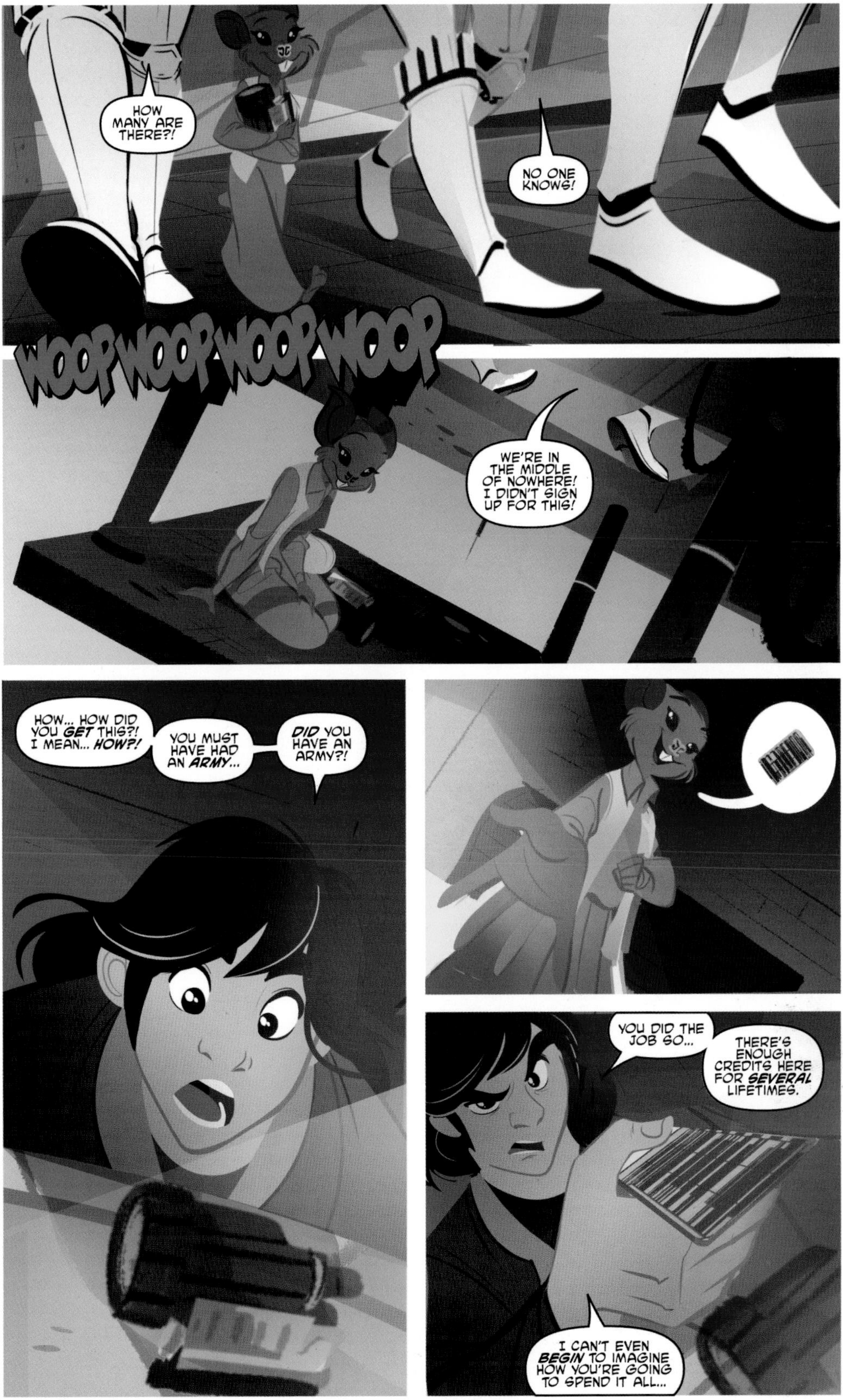
HOW MANY ARE THERE?!
NO ONE KNOWS!
WOOPWOOPWOOPWOOP
WE'RE IN THE MIDDLE OF NOWHERE! I DIDN'T SIGN UP FOR THIS!
HOW... HOW DID YOU GET THIS?! I MEAN... HOW?!
YOU MUST HAVE HAD AN ARMY...
DID YOU HAVE AN ARMY?!
YOU DID THE JOB SO...
THERE'S ENOUGH CREDITS HERE FOR SEVERAL LIFETIMES.
I CAN'T EVEN BEGIN TO IMAGINE HOW YOU'RE GOING TO SPEND IT ALL...

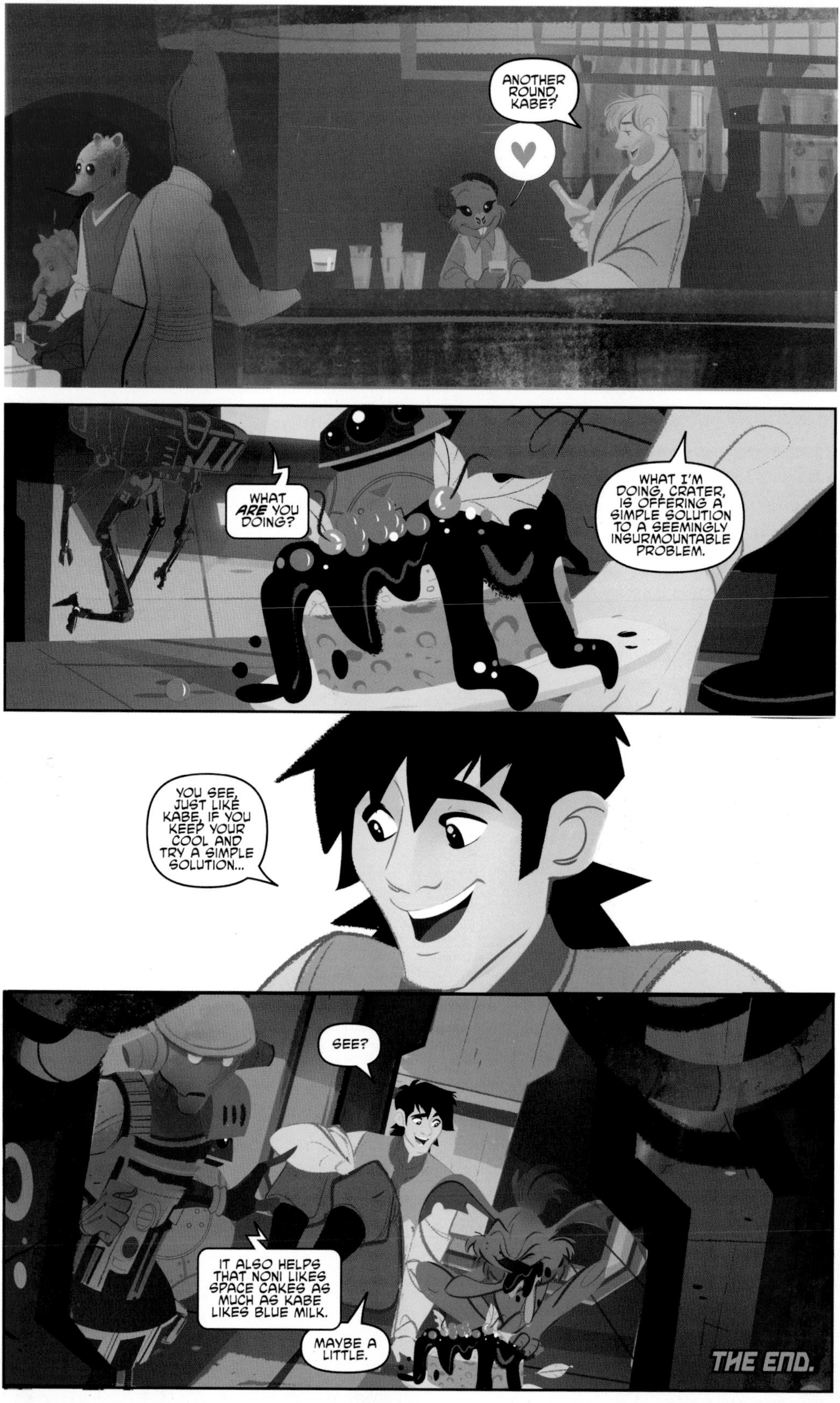
ANOTHER ROUND, KABE?
WHAT ARE YOU DOING?
WHAT I'M DOING, CRATER, IS OFFERING A SIMPLE SOLUTION TO A SEEMINGLY INSURMOUNTABLE PROBLEM.
YOU SEE, JUST LIKE KABE, IF YOU KEEP YOUR COOL AND TRY A SIMPLE SOLUTION...
SEE?
IT ALSO HELPS THAT NONI LIKES SPACE CAKES AS MUCH AS KABE LIKES BLUE MILK.
MAYBE A LITTLE.
THE END.

TALES FROM WILD SPACE

A Tauntaun Tail

WRITER
JON WATERHOUSE

ARTIST
TONY FLEECS

COLOR FLATTER
LAUREN PERRY

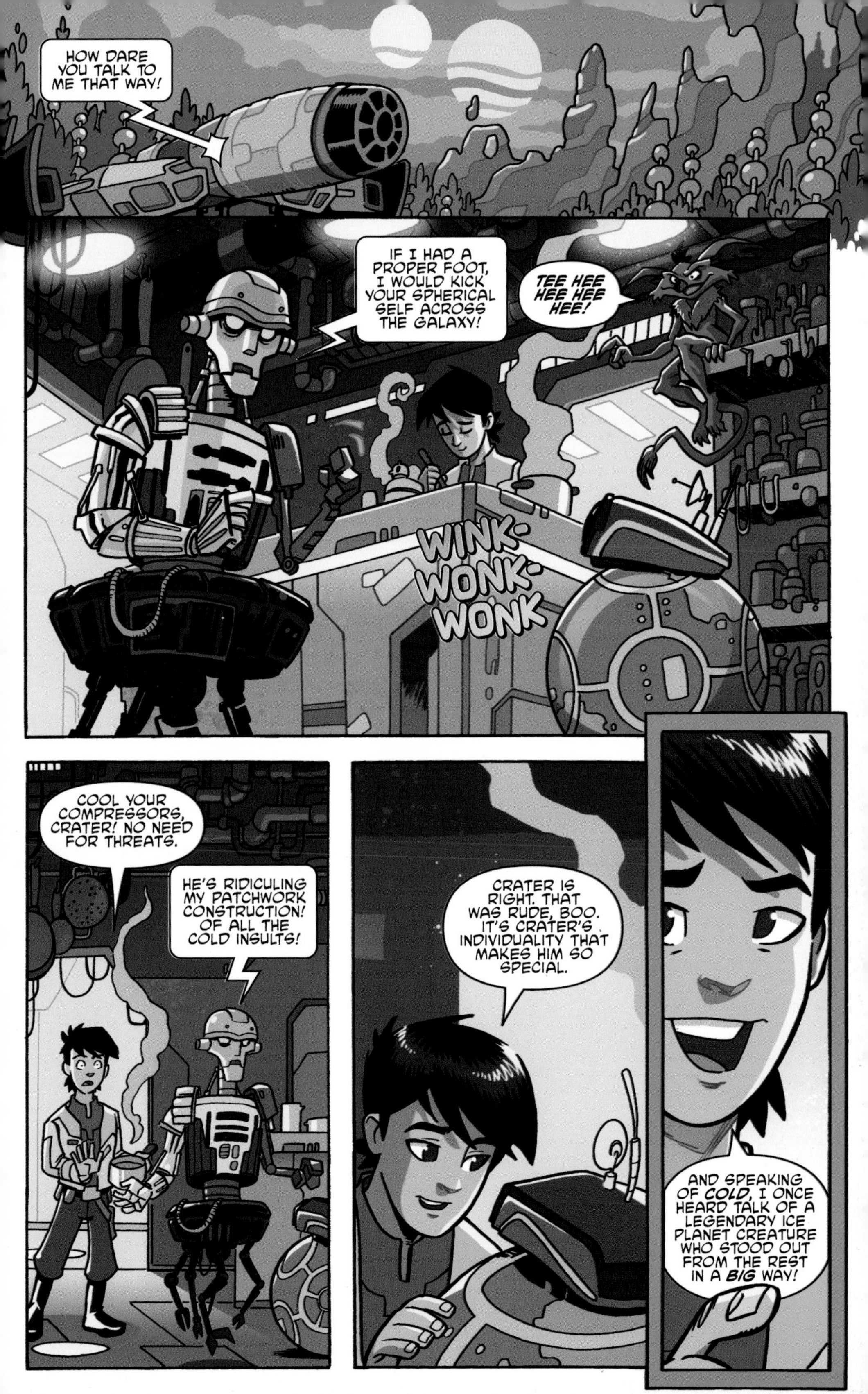
HOW DARE YOU TALK TO ME THAT WAY!
IF I HAD A PROPER FOOT, I WOULD KICK YOUR SPHERICAL SELF ACROSS THE GALAXY!
TEE HEE HEE HEE HEE!
WINK-WONK-WONK
COOL YOUR COMPRESSORS, CRATER! NO NEED FOR THREATS.
HE'S RIDICULING MY PATCHWORK CONSTRUCTION! OF ALL THE COLD INSULTS!
CRATER IS RIGHT. THAT WAS RUDE, BOO. IT'S CRATER'S INDIVIDUALITY THAT MAKES HIM SO SPECIAL.
AND SPEAKING OF COLD, I ONCE HEARD TALK OF A LEGENDARY ICE PLANET CREATURE WHO STOOD OUT FROM THE REST IN A BIG WAY!

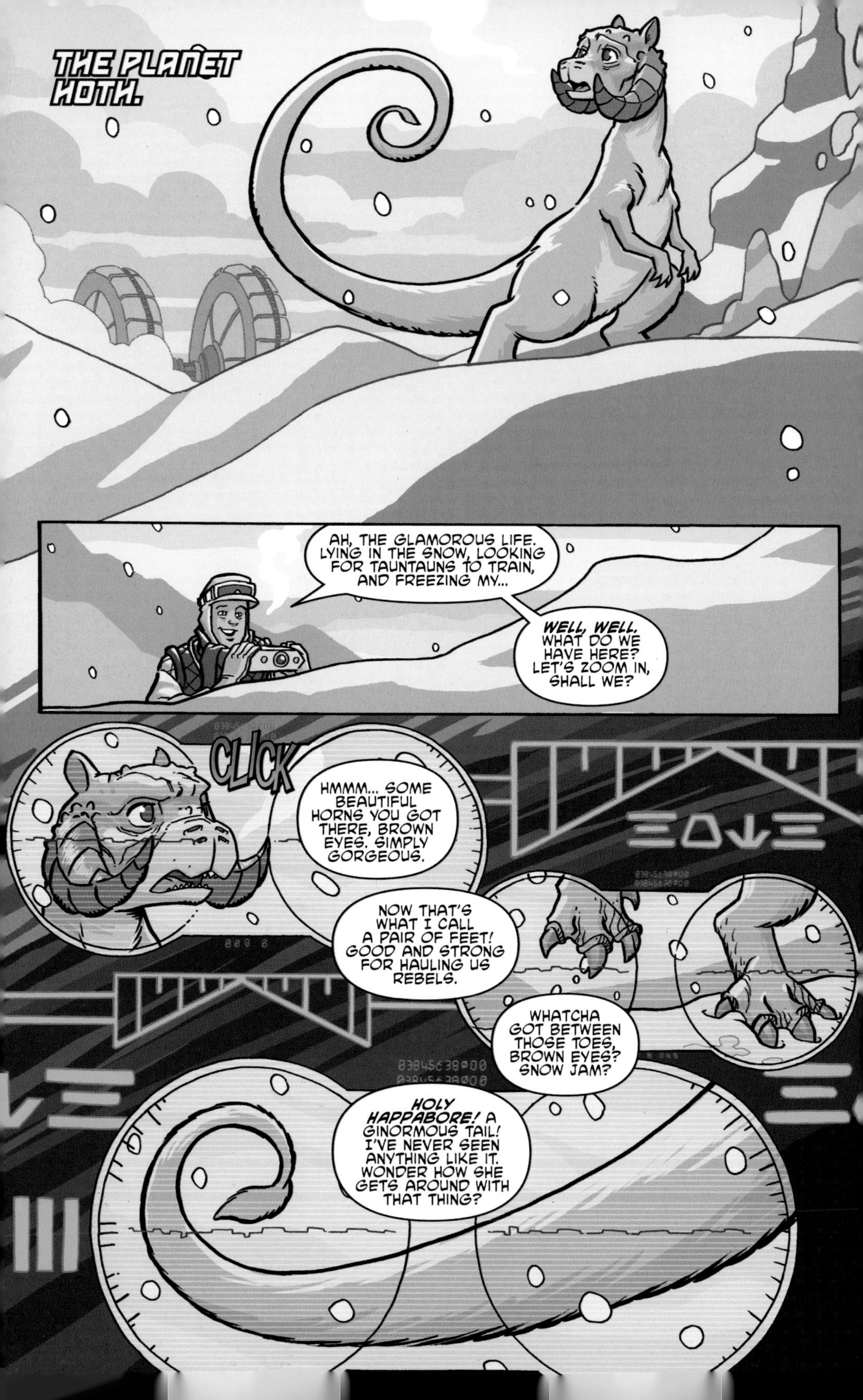
THE PLANET HOTH.
AH, THE GLAMOROUS LIFE. LYING IN THE SNOW, LOOKING FOR TAUNTAUNS TO TRAIN, AND FREEZING MY...
WELL, WELL. WHAT DO WE HAVE HERE? LET'S ZOOM IN, SHALL WE?
CLICK
HMMM... SOME BEAUTIFUL HORNS YOU GOT THERE, BROWN EYES. SIMPLY GORGEOUS.
NOW THAT'S WHAT I CALL A PAIR OF FEET! GOOD AND STRONG FOR HAULING US REBELS.
WHATCHA GOT BETWEEN THOSE TOES, BROWN EYES? SNOW JAM?
HOLY HAPPABORE! A GINORMOUS TAIL! I'VE NEVER SEEN ANYTHING LIKE IT. WONDER HOW SHE GETS AROUND WITH THAT THING?

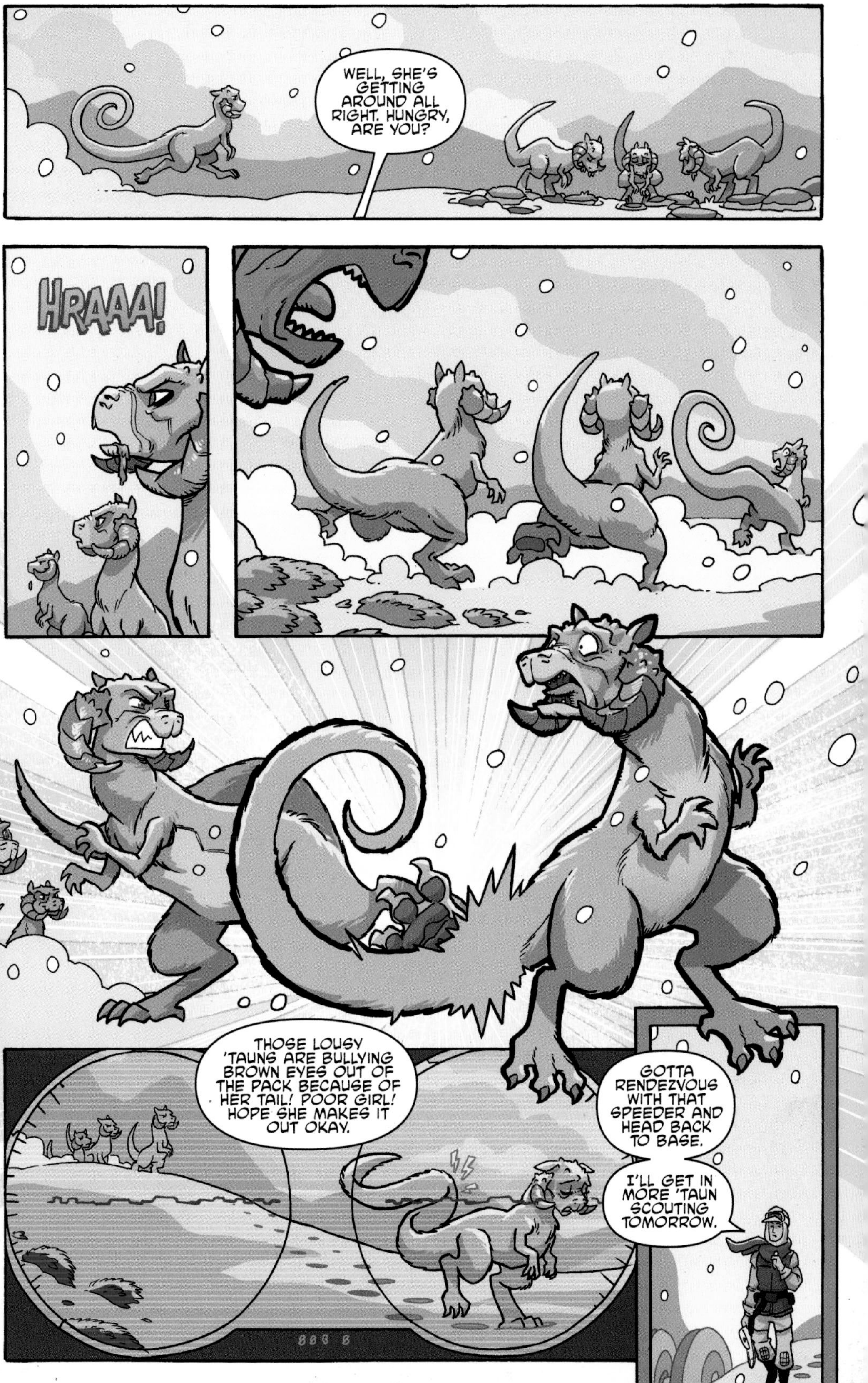
WELL, SHE'S GETTING AROUND ALL RIGHT. HUNGRY, ARE YOU?
HRAAA!
THOSE LOUSY 'TAUNS ARE BULLYING BROWN EYES OUT OF THE PACK BECAUSE OF HER TAIL! POOR GIRL! HOPE SHE MAKES IT OUT OKAY.
GOTTA RENDEZVOUS WITH THAT SPEEDER AND HEAD BACK TO BASE.
I'LL GET IN MORE 'TAUN SCOUTING TOMORROW.

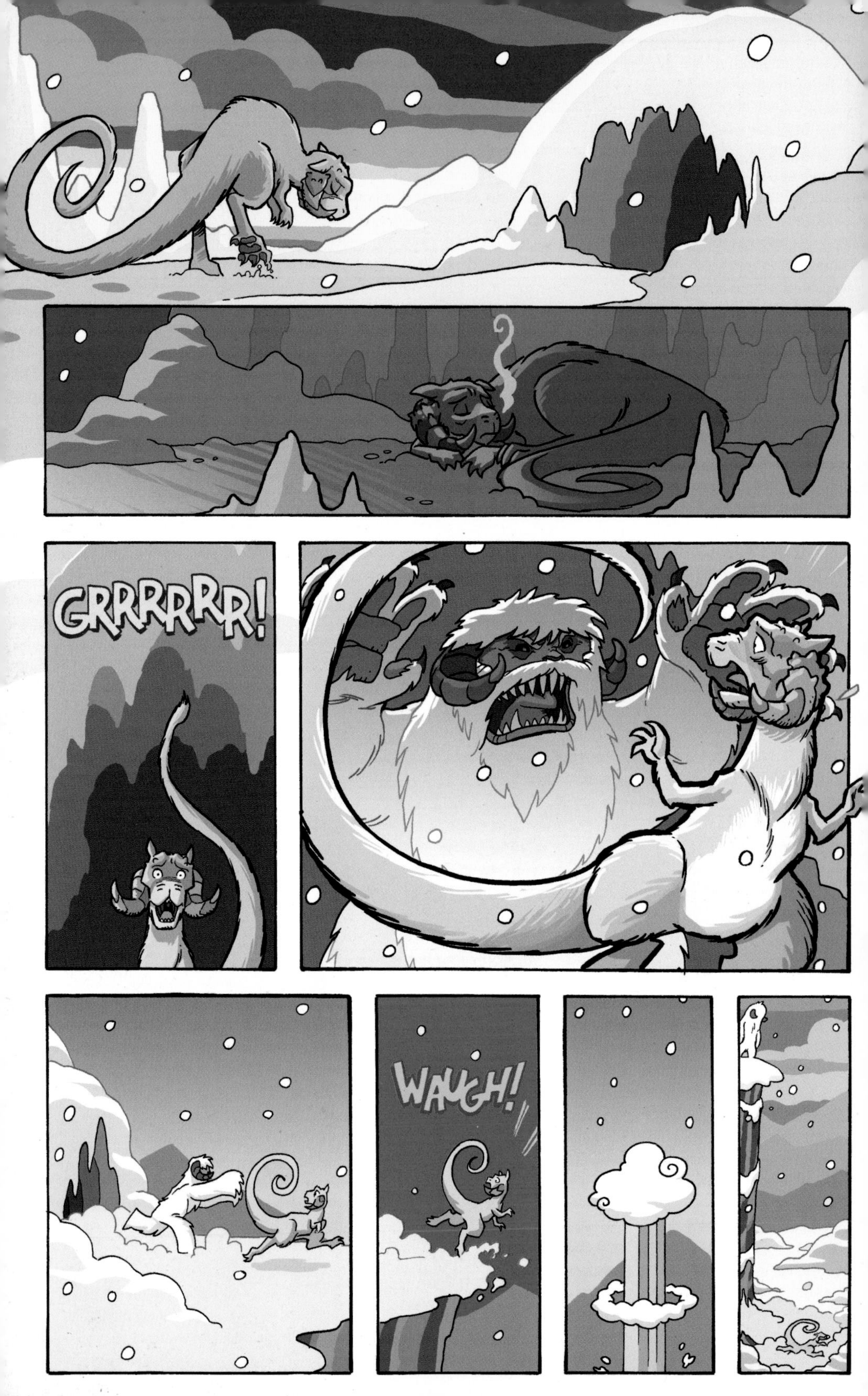
GRRRRRR!
WAUGH!

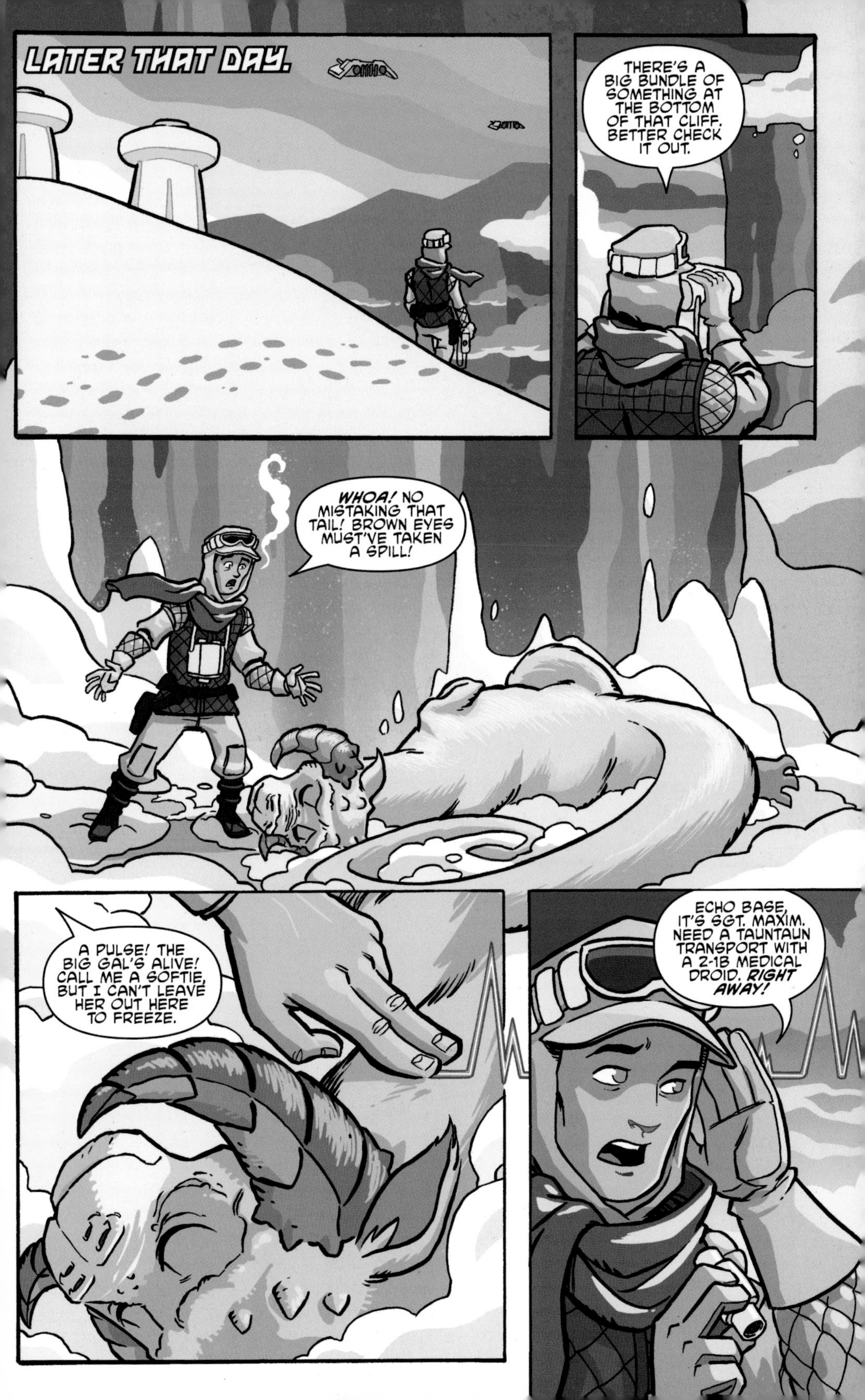
LATER THAT DAY.
THERE'S A BIG BUNDLE OF SOMETHING AT THE BOTTOM OF THAT CLIFF. BETTER CHECK IT OUT.
WHOA! NO MISTAKING THAT TAIL! BROWN EYES MUST'VE TAKEN A SPILL!
A PULSE! THE BIG GAL'S ALIVE! CALL ME A SOFTIE, BUT I CAN'T LEAVE HER OUT HERE TO FREEZE.
ECHO BASE, IT'S SGT. MAXIM. NEED A TAUNTAUN TRANSPORT WITH A 2-1B MEDICAL DROID. RIGHT AWAY!

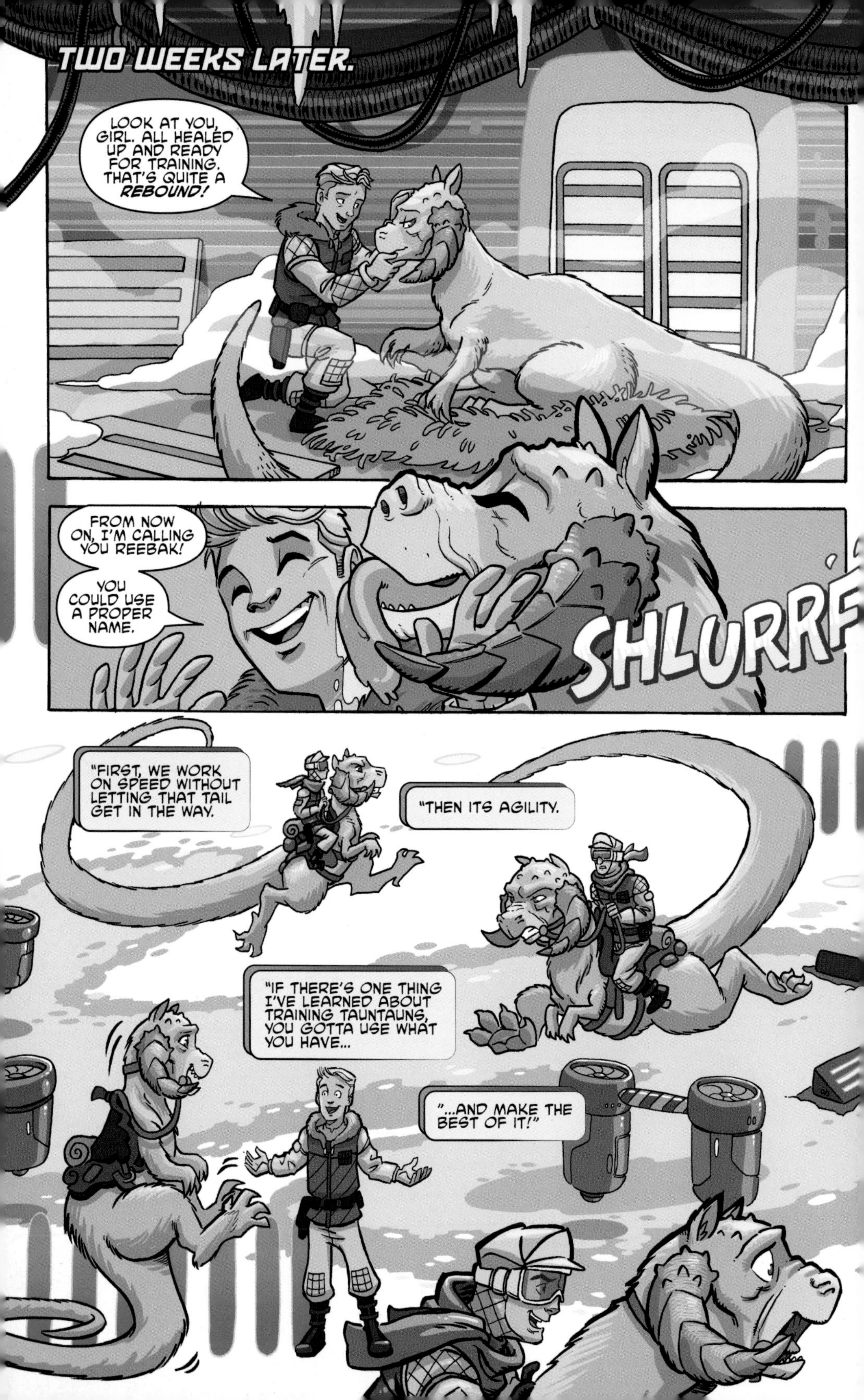
TWO WEEKS LATER.
LOOK AT YOU, GIRL. ALL HEALED UP AND READY FOR TRAINING. THAT'S QUITE A REBOUND!
FROM NOW ON, I'M CALLING YOU REEBAK!
YOU COULD USE A PROPER NAME.
SHLURRF
"FIRST, WE WORK ON SPEED WITHOUT LETTING THAT TAIL GET IN THE WAY.
"THEN ITS AGILITY.
"IF THERE'S ONE THING I'VE LEARNED ABOUT TRAINING TAUNTAUNS, YOU GOTTA USE WHAT YOU HAVE...
"...AND MAKE THE BEST OF IT!"

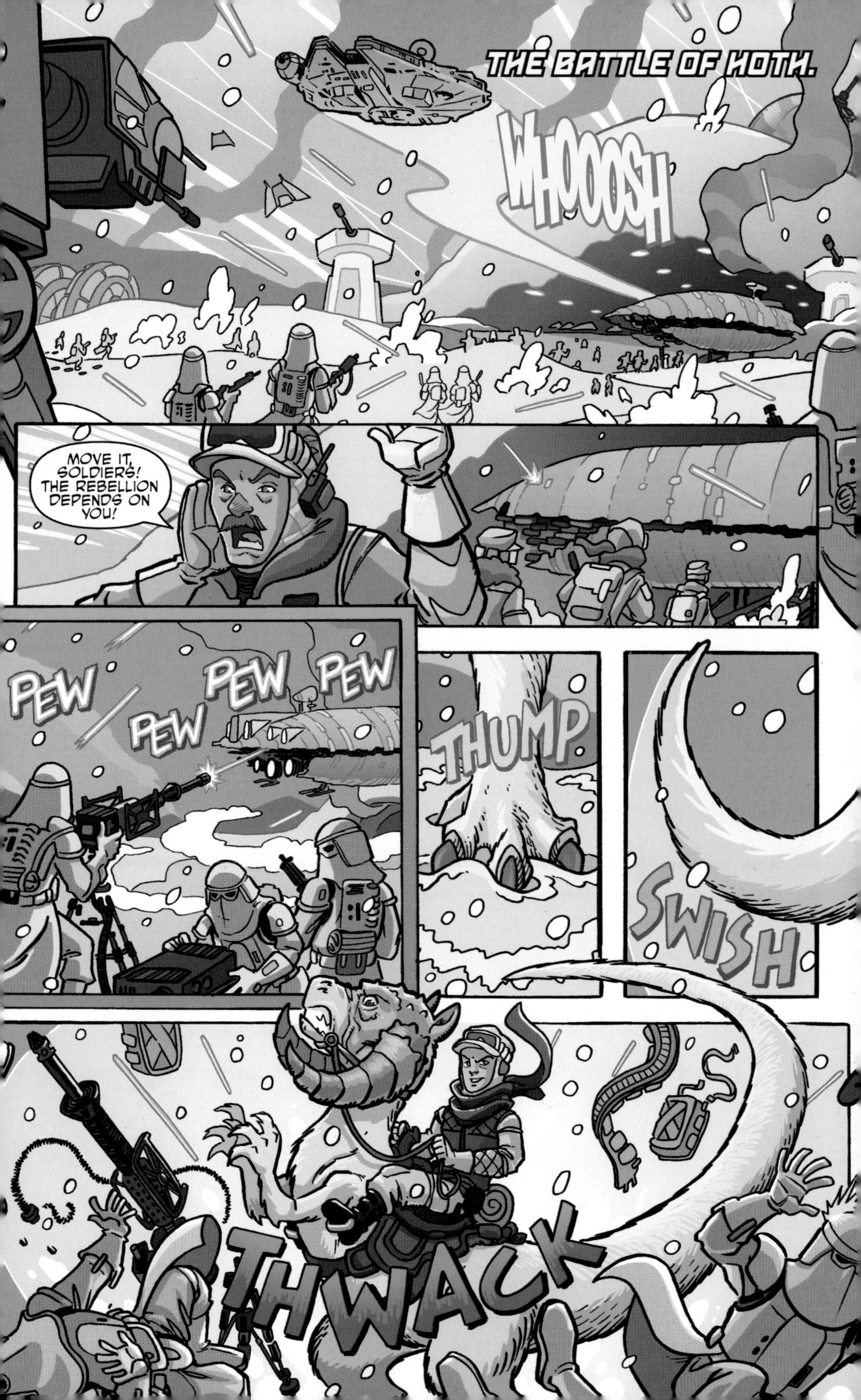
THE BATTLE OF HOTH.
WHOOOSH
MOVE IT, SOLDIERS! THE REBELLION DEPENDS ON YOU!
PEW
PEW
PEW
PEW
THUMP
SWISH
THWACK

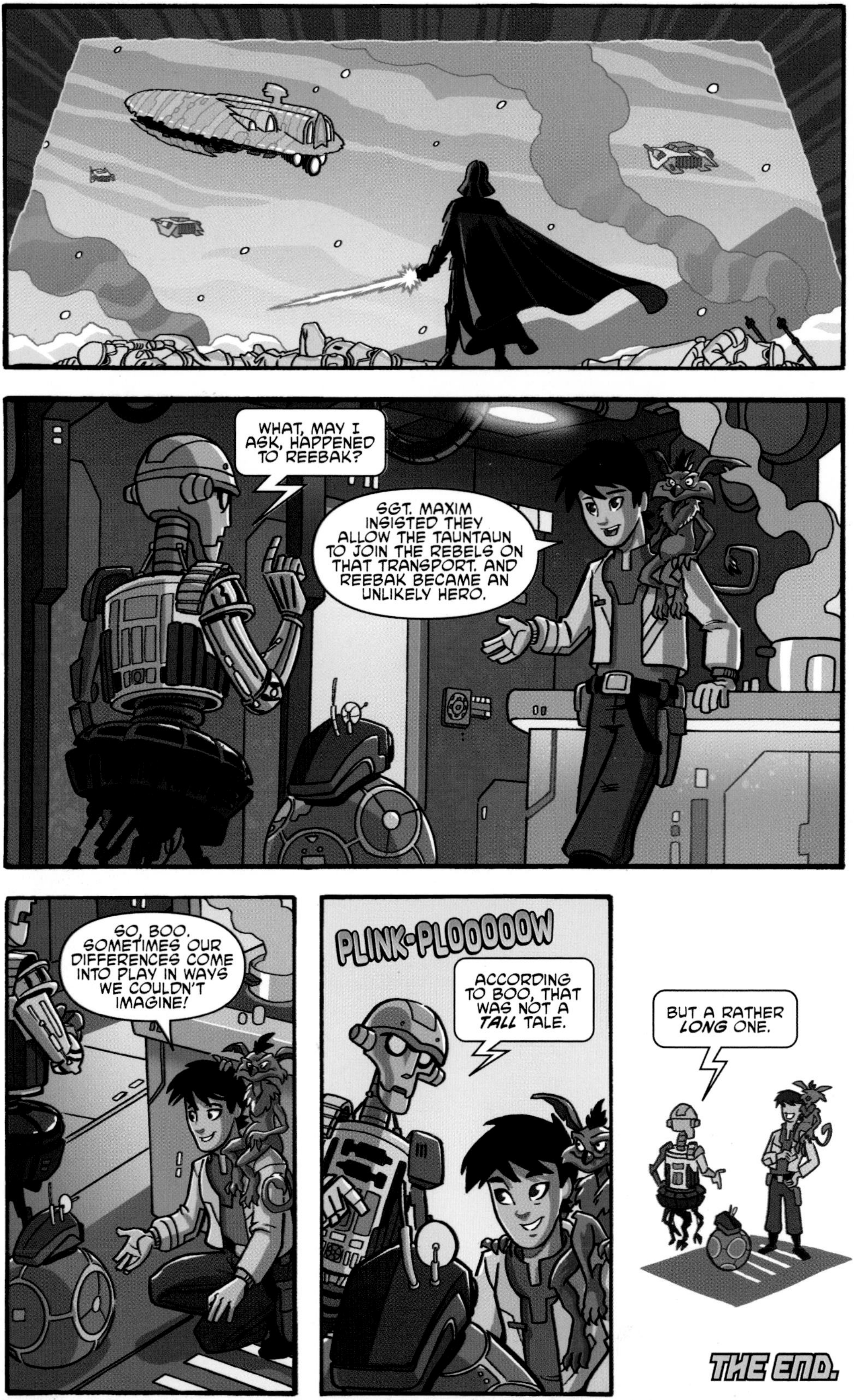
WHAT, MAY I ASK, HAPPENED TO REEBAK?
SGT. MAXIM INSISTED THEY ALLOW THE TAUNTAUN TO JOIN THE REBELS ON THAT TRANSPORT. AND REEBAK BECAME AN UNLIKELY HERO.
SO, BOO. SOMETIMES OUR DIFFERENCES COME INTO PLAY IN WAYS WE COULDN'T IMAGINE!
PLINK-PLOOOOOW
ACCORDING TO BOO, THAT WAS NOT A *TALL* TALE.
BUT A RATHER *LONG* ONE.
THE END.

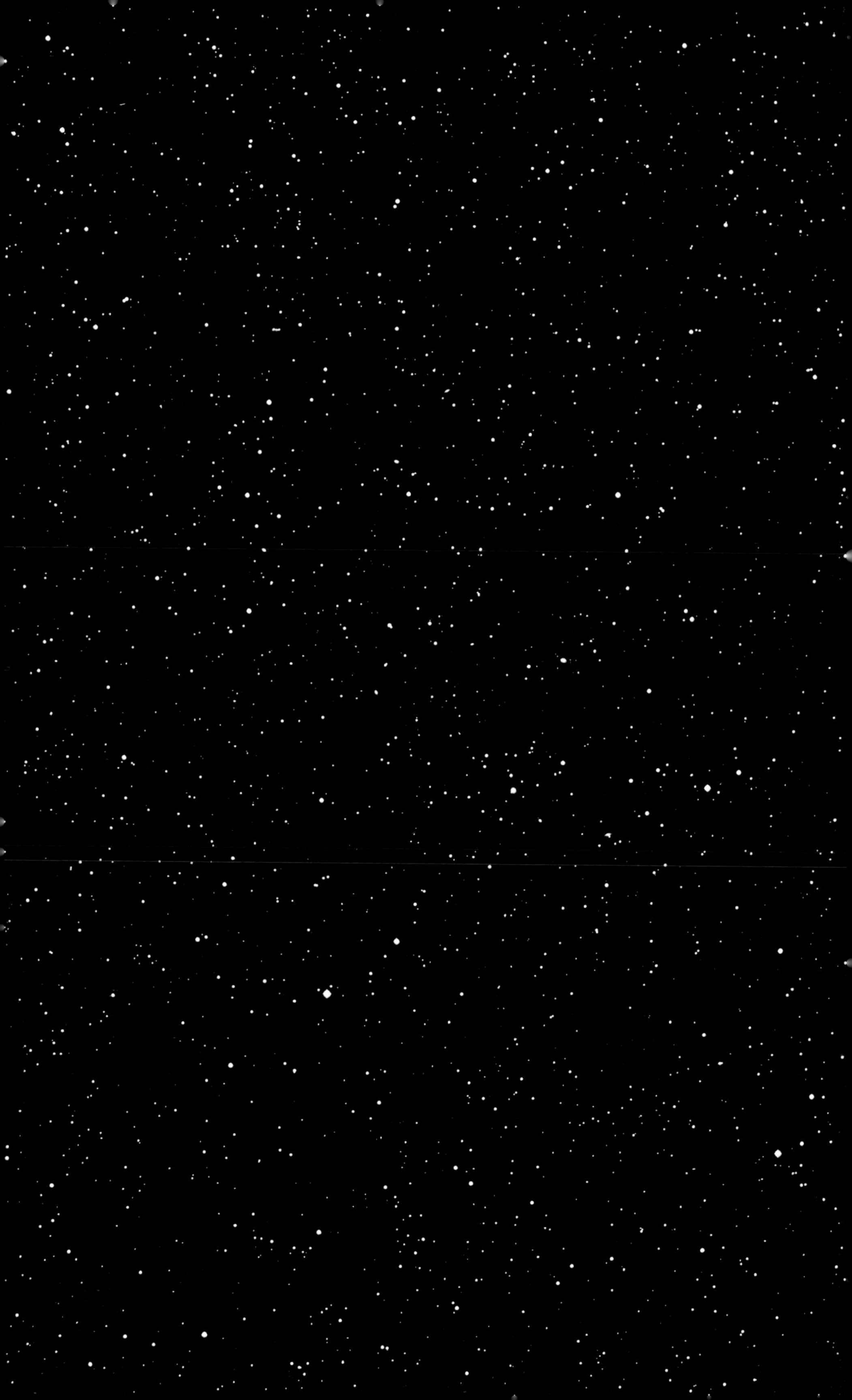

TALES FROM WILD SPACE

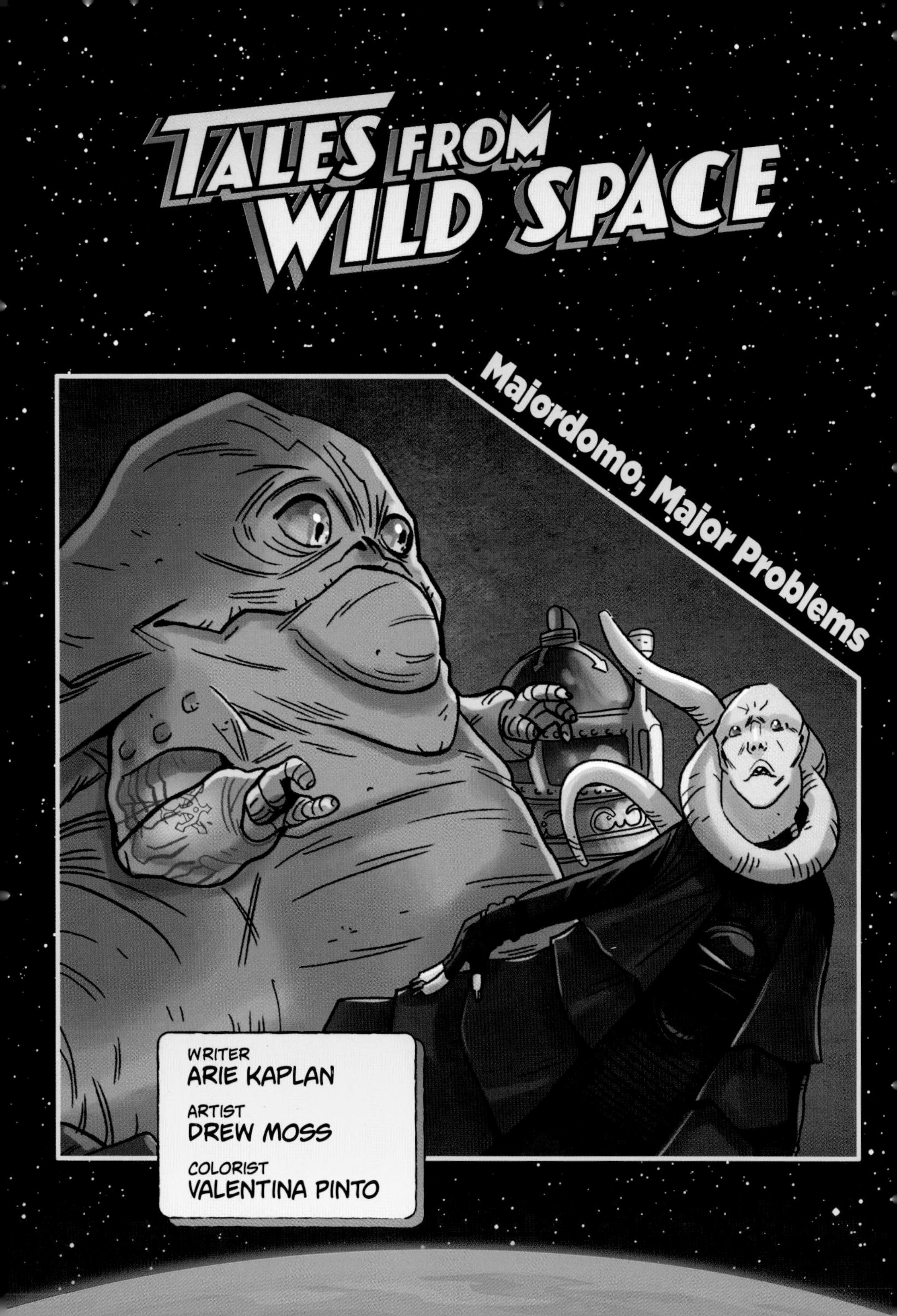
Majordomo; Major Problems

WRITER
ARIE KAPLAN
ARTIST
DREW MOSS
COLORIST
VALENTINA PINTO

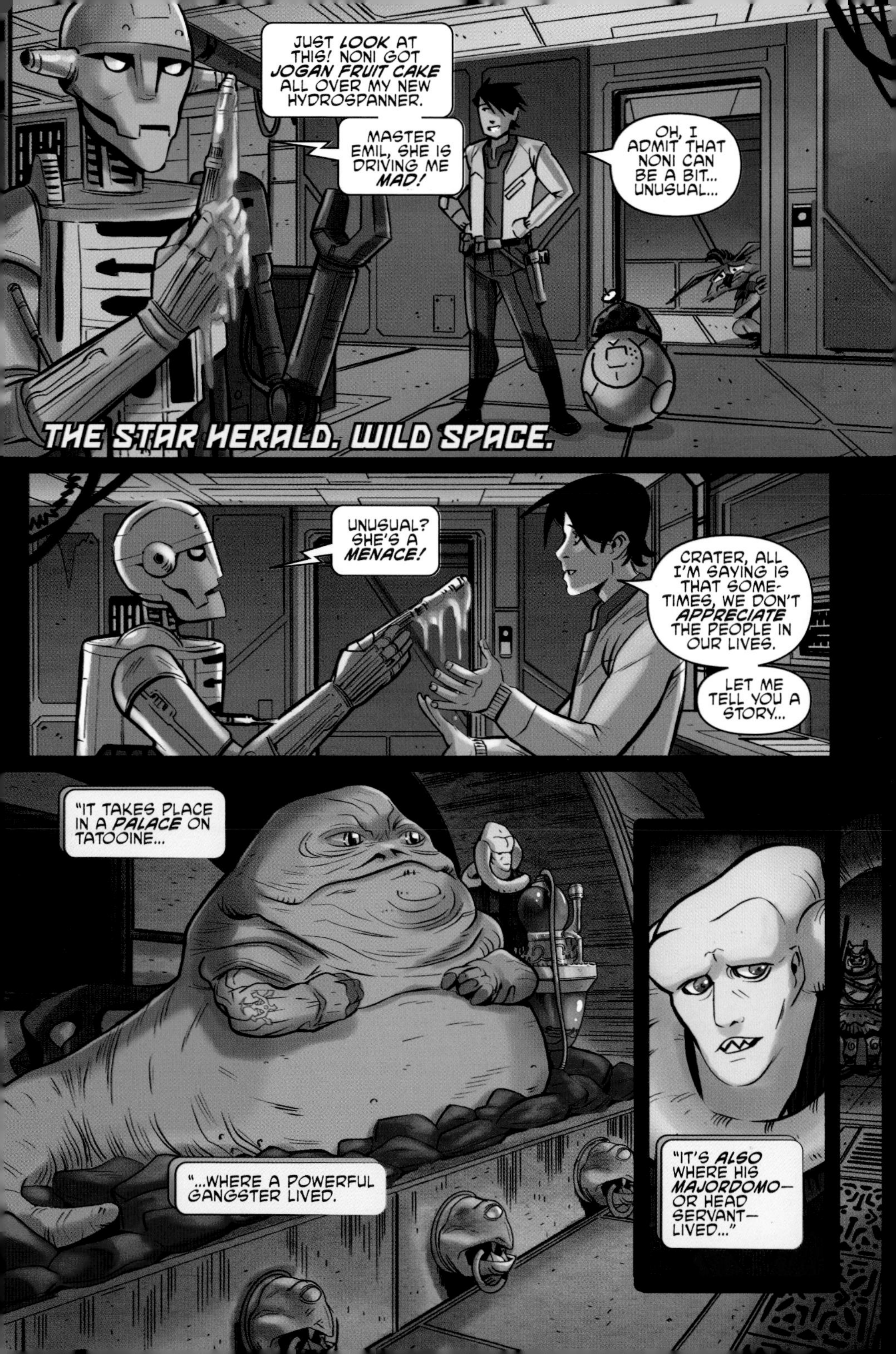
JUST LOOK AT THIS! NONI GOT JOGAN FRUIT CAKE ALL OVER MY NEW HYDROSPANNER.
MASTER EMIL, SHE IS DRIVING ME MAD!
OH, I ADMIT THAT NONI CAN BE A BIT... UNUSUAL...
THE STAR HERALD. WILD SPACE.
UNUSUAL? SHE'S A MENACE!
CRATER, ALL I'M SAYING IS THAT SOME-TIMES, WE DON'T APPRECIATE THE PEOPLE IN OUR LIVES.
LET ME TELL YOU A STORY...
"IT TAKES PLACE IN A PALACE ON TATOOINE...
"...WHERE A POWERFUL GANGSTER LIVED.
"IT'S ALSO WHERE HIS MAJORDOMO—OR HEAD SERVANT—LIVED..."

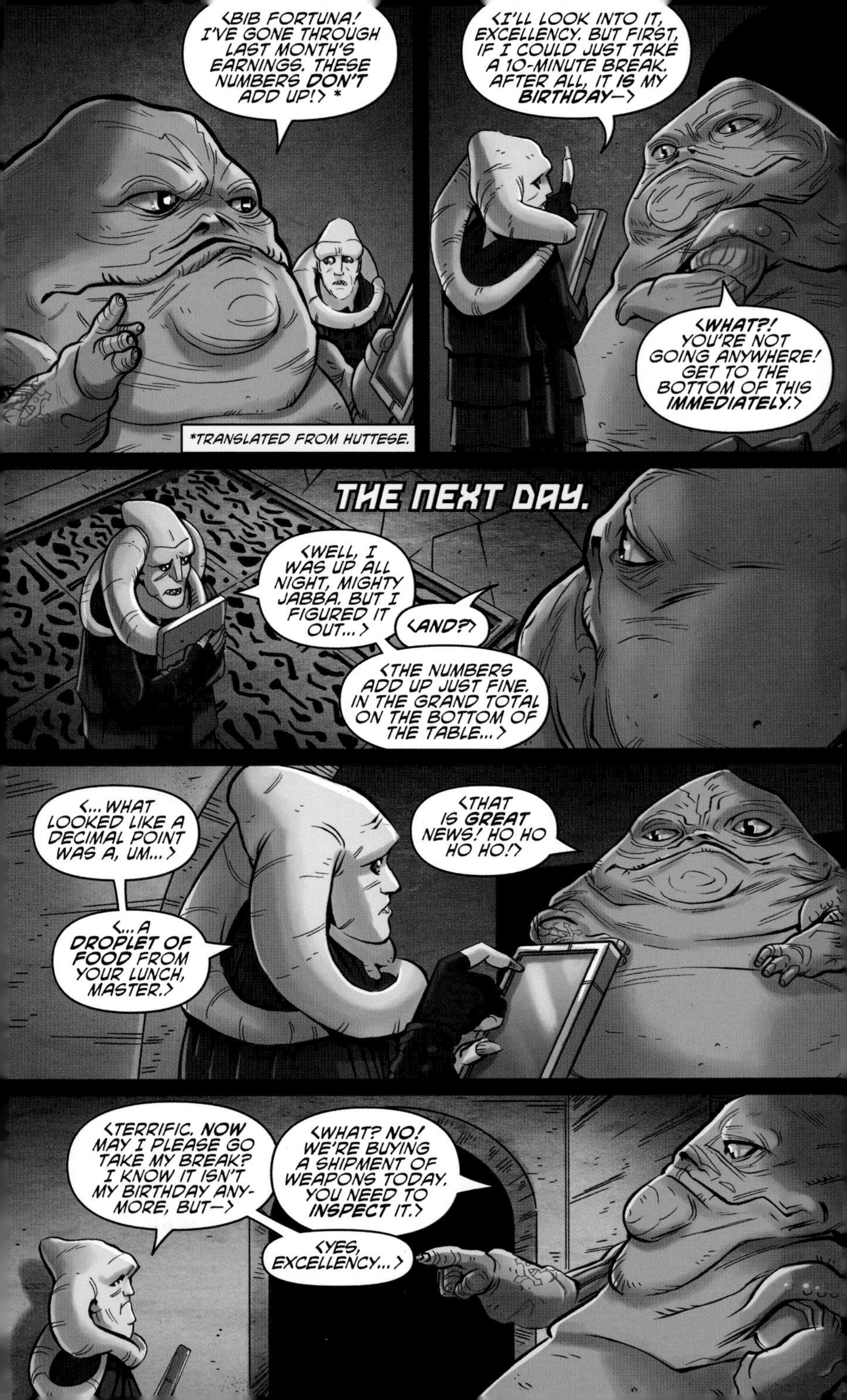
<BIB FORTUNA! I'VE GONE THROUGH LAST MONTH'S EARNINGS. THESE NUMBERS **DON'T** ADD UP!> *
*TRANSLATED FROM HUTTESE.
<I'LL LOOK INTO IT, EXCELLENCY. BUT FIRST, IF I COULD JUST TAKE A 10-MINUTE BREAK. AFTER ALL, IT **IS** MY **BIRTHDAY**—>
<**WHAT?!** YOU'RE NOT GOING ANYWHERE! GET TO THE BOTTOM OF THIS **IMMEDIATELY.**>
THE NEXT DAY.
<WELL, I WAS UP ALL NIGHT, MIGHTY JABBA. BUT I FIGURED IT OUT...>
<**AND?**>
<THE NUMBERS ADD UP JUST FINE. IN THE GRAND TOTAL ON THE BOTTOM OF THE TABLE...>
<...WHAT LOOKED LIKE A DECIMAL POINT WAS A, UM...>
<...A **DROPLET OF FOOD** FROM YOUR LUNCH, MASTER.>
<THAT IS **GREAT** NEWS! HO HO HO HO!>
<TERRIFIC. **NOW** MAY I PLEASE GO TAKE MY BREAK? I KNOW IT ISN'T MY BIRTHDAY ANY-MORE, BUT—>
<WHAT? **NO!** WE'RE BUYING A SHIPMENT OF WEAPONS TODAY. YOU NEED TO **INSPECT** IT.>
<YES, EXCELLENCY...>

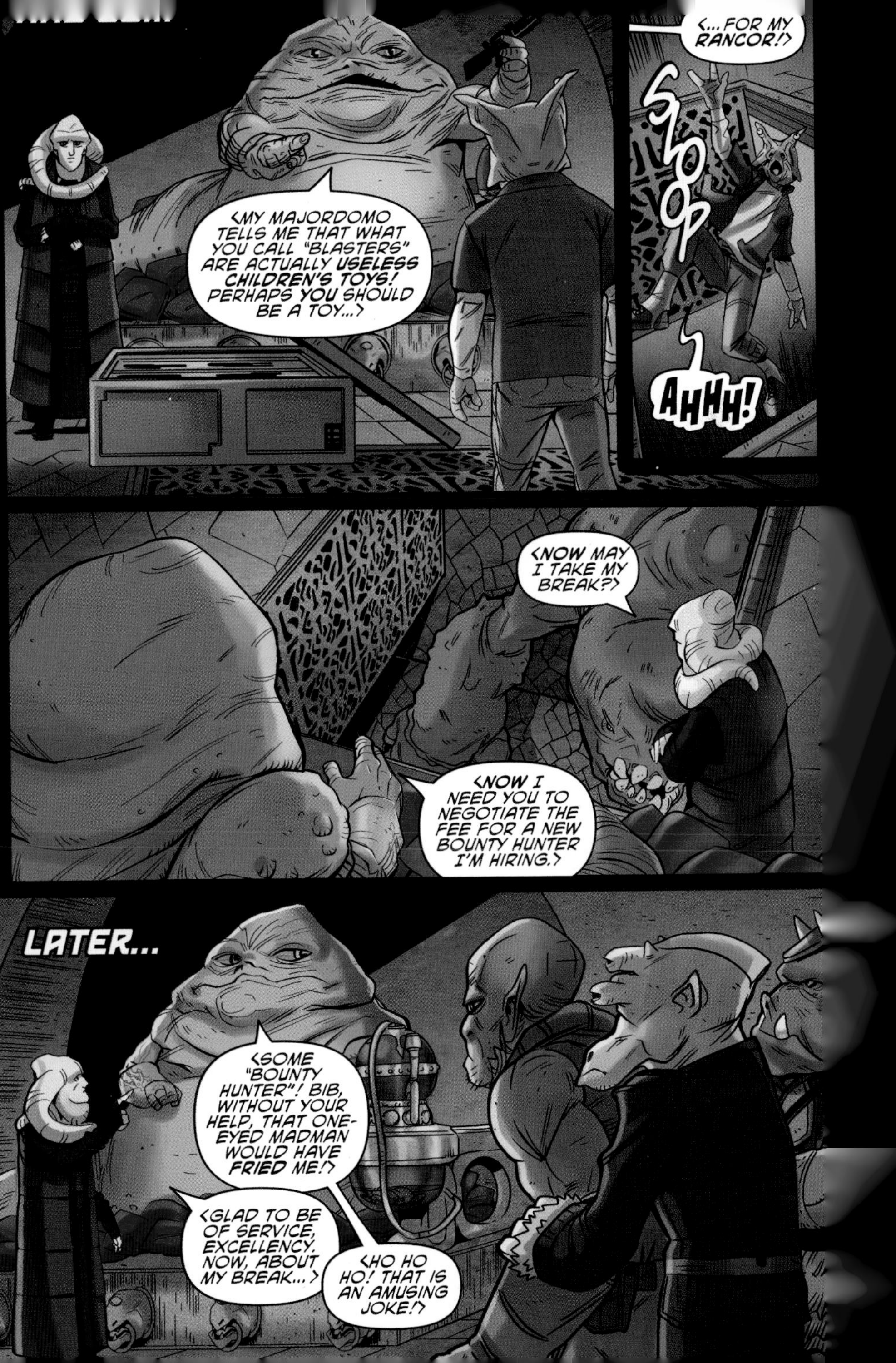
<MY MAJORDOMO TELLS ME THAT WHAT YOU CALL "BLASTERS" ARE ACTUALLY USELESS CHILDREN'S TOYS! PERHAPS YOU SHOULD BE A TOY...>
<...FOR MY RANCOR!>
SHLOOP
AHHH!
<NOW MAY I TAKE MY BREAK?>
<NOW I NEED YOU TO NEGOTIATE THE FEE FOR A NEW BOUNTY HUNTER I'M HIRING.>
LATER...
<SOME "BOUNTY HUNTER"! BIB, WITHOUT YOUR HELP, THAT ONE-EYED MADMAN WOULD HAVE FRIED ME!>
<GLAD TO BE OF SERVICE, EXCELLENCY. NOW, ABOUT MY BREAK...>
<HO HO HO! THAT IS AN AMUSING JOKE!>

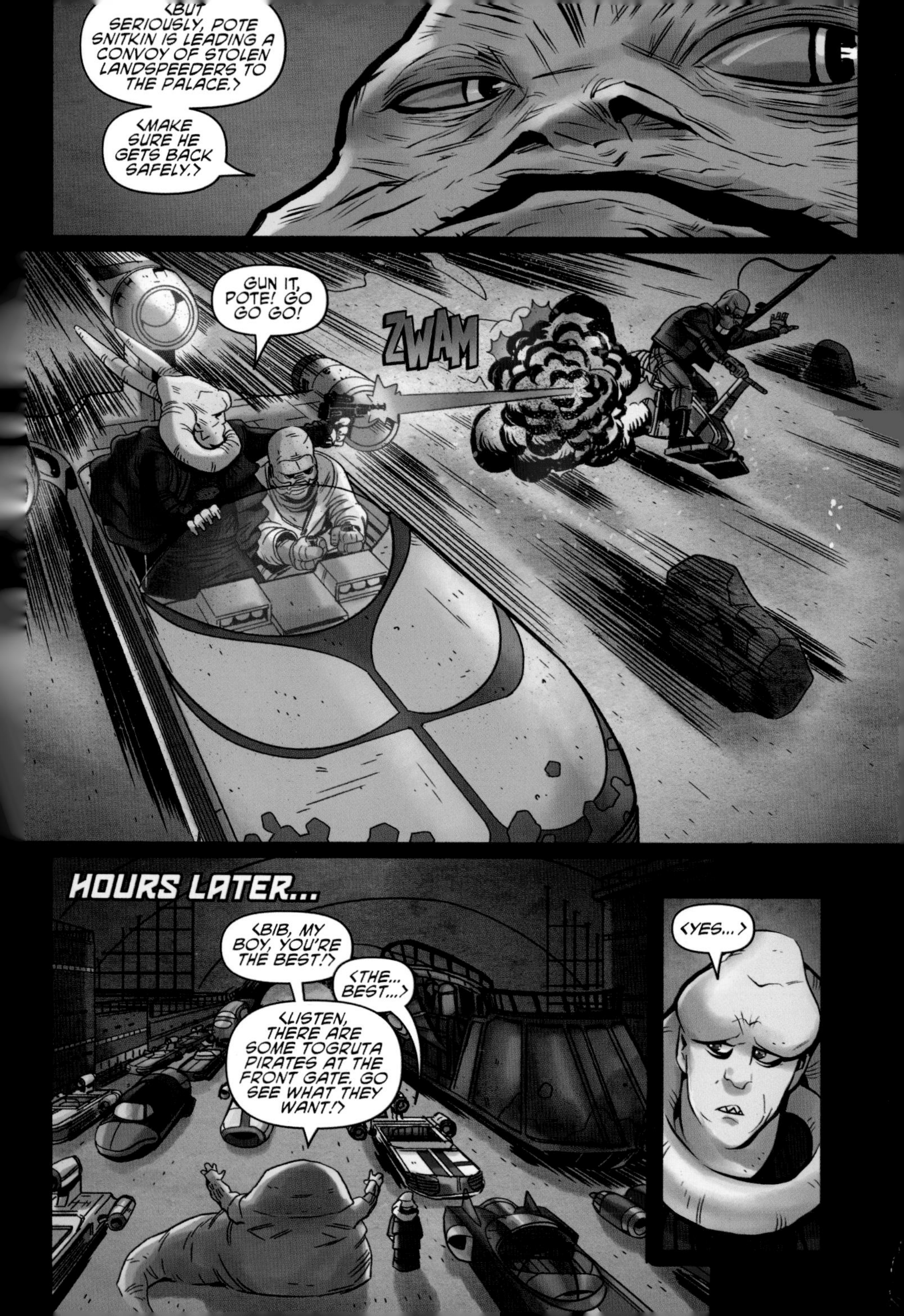
<BUT SERIOUSLY, POTE SNITKIN IS LEADING A CONVOY OF STOLEN LANDSPEEDERS TO THE PALACE.>
<MAKE SURE HE GETS BACK SAFELY.>
GUN IT, POTE! GO GO GO!
ZWAM
HOURS LATER...
<BIB, MY BOY, YOU'RE THE BEST!>
<THE... BEST...>
<LISTEN, THERE ARE SOME TOGRUTA PIRATES AT THE FRONT GATE. GO SEE WHAT THEY WANT!>
<YES...>

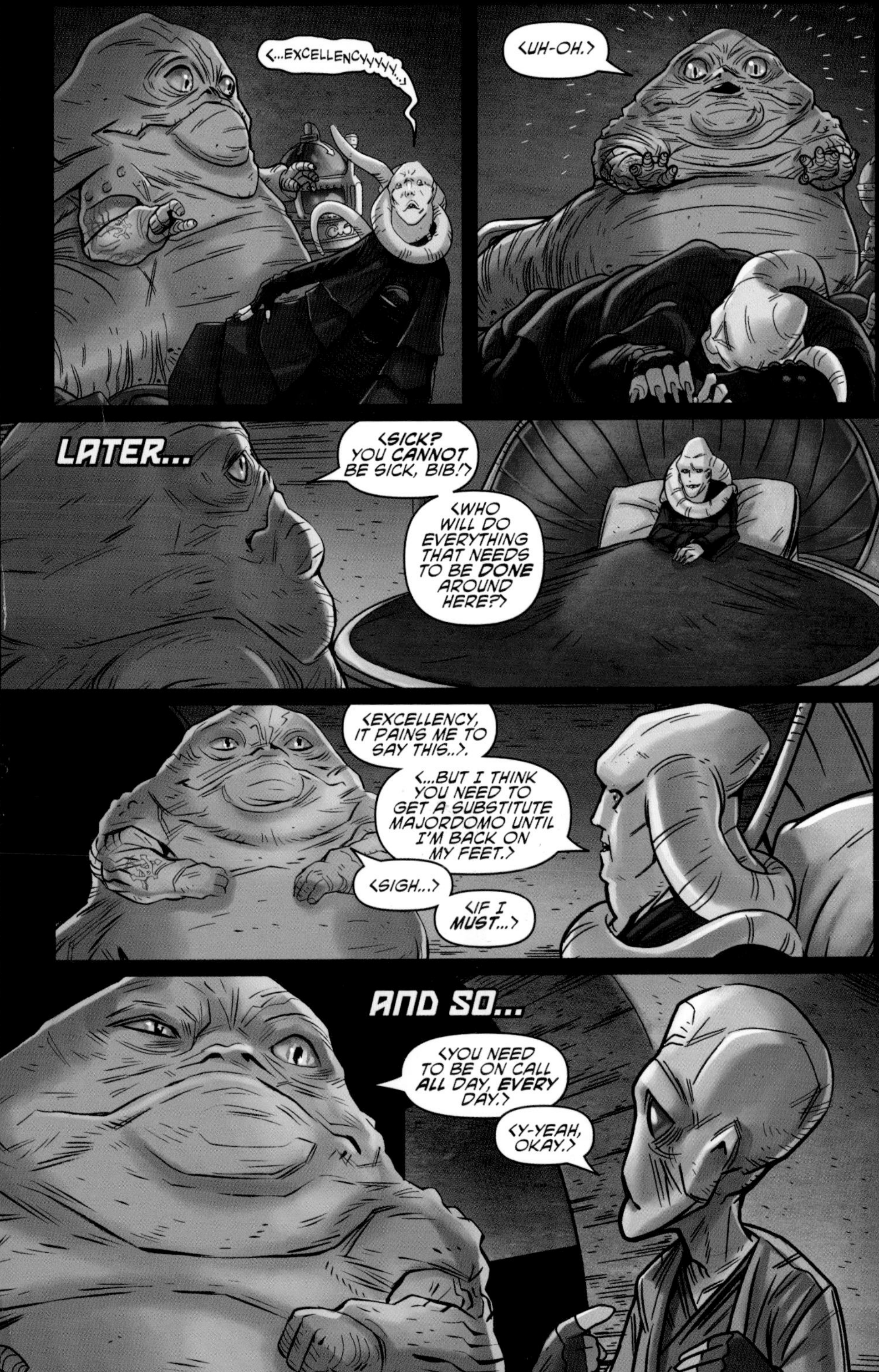

<...EXCELLENCYYYYYY...>
<UH-OH.>
LATER...
<SICK? YOU CANNOT BE SICK, BIB!>
<WHO WILL DO EVERYTHING THAT NEEDS TO BE DONE AROUND HERE?>
<EXCELLENCY, IT PAINS ME TO SAY THIS...>
<...BUT I THINK YOU NEED TO GET A SUBSTITUTE MAJORDOMO UNTIL I'M BACK ON MY FEET.>
<SIGH...>
<IF I MUST...>
AND SO...
<YOU NEED TO BE ON CALL ALL DAY, EVERY DAY.>
<Y-YEAH, OKAY.>

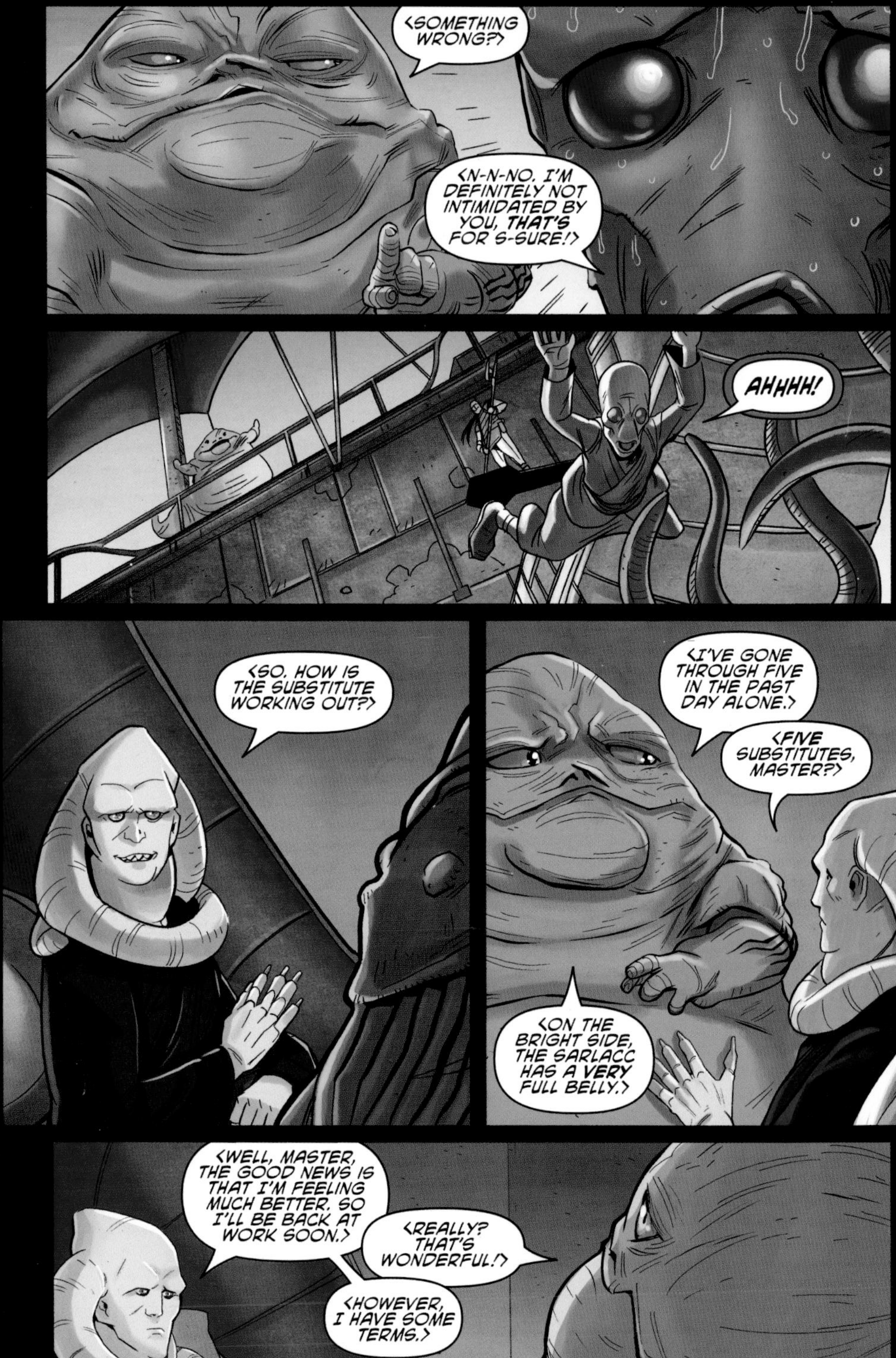

<SOMETHING WRONG?>
<N-N-NO. I'M DEFINITELY NOT INTIMIDATED BY YOU, THAT'S FOR S-SURE!>
AHHHH!
<SO. HOW IS THE SUBSTITUTE WORKING OUT?>
<I'VE GONE THROUGH FIVE IN THE PAST DAY ALONE.>
<FIVE SUBSTITUTES, MASTER?>
<ON THE BRIGHT SIDE, THE SARLACC HAS A VERY FULL BELLY.>
<WELL, MASTER, THE GOOD NEWS IS THAT I'M FEELING MUCH BETTER. SO I'LL BE BACK AT WORK SOON.>
<REALLY? THAT'S WONDERFUL!>
<HOWEVER, I HAVE SOME TERMS.>

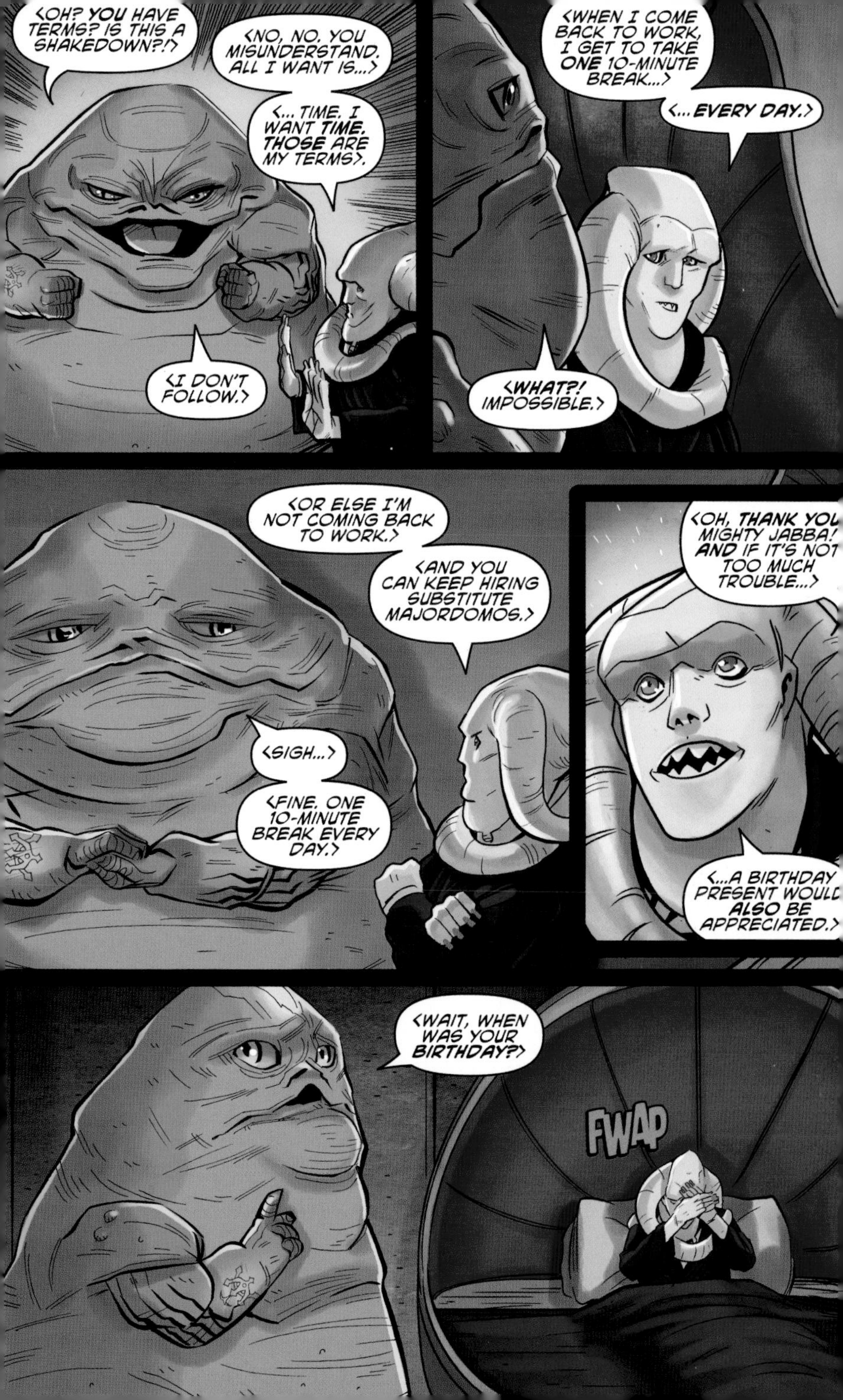

<OH? YOU HAVE TERMS? IS THIS A SHAKEDOWN?!>
<NO, NO. YOU MISUNDERSTAND. ALL I WANT IS...>
<... TIME. I WANT TIME. THOSE ARE MY TERMS>.
<I DON'T FOLLOW.>
<WHEN I COME BACK TO WORK, I GET TO TAKE ONE 10-MINUTE BREAK...>
<... EVERY DAY.>
<WHAT?! IMPOSSIBLE.>
<OR ELSE I'M NOT COMING BACK TO WORK.>
<AND YOU CAN KEEP HIRING SUBSTITUTE MAJORDOMOS.>
<SIGH...>
<FINE. ONE 10-MINUTE BREAK EVERY DAY.>
<OH, THANK YOU MIGHTY JABBA! AND IF IT'S NOT TOO MUCH TROUBLE...>
<...A BIRTHDAY PRESENT WOULD ALSO BE APPRECIATED.>
<WAIT, WHEN WAS YOUR BIRTHDAY?>
FWAP

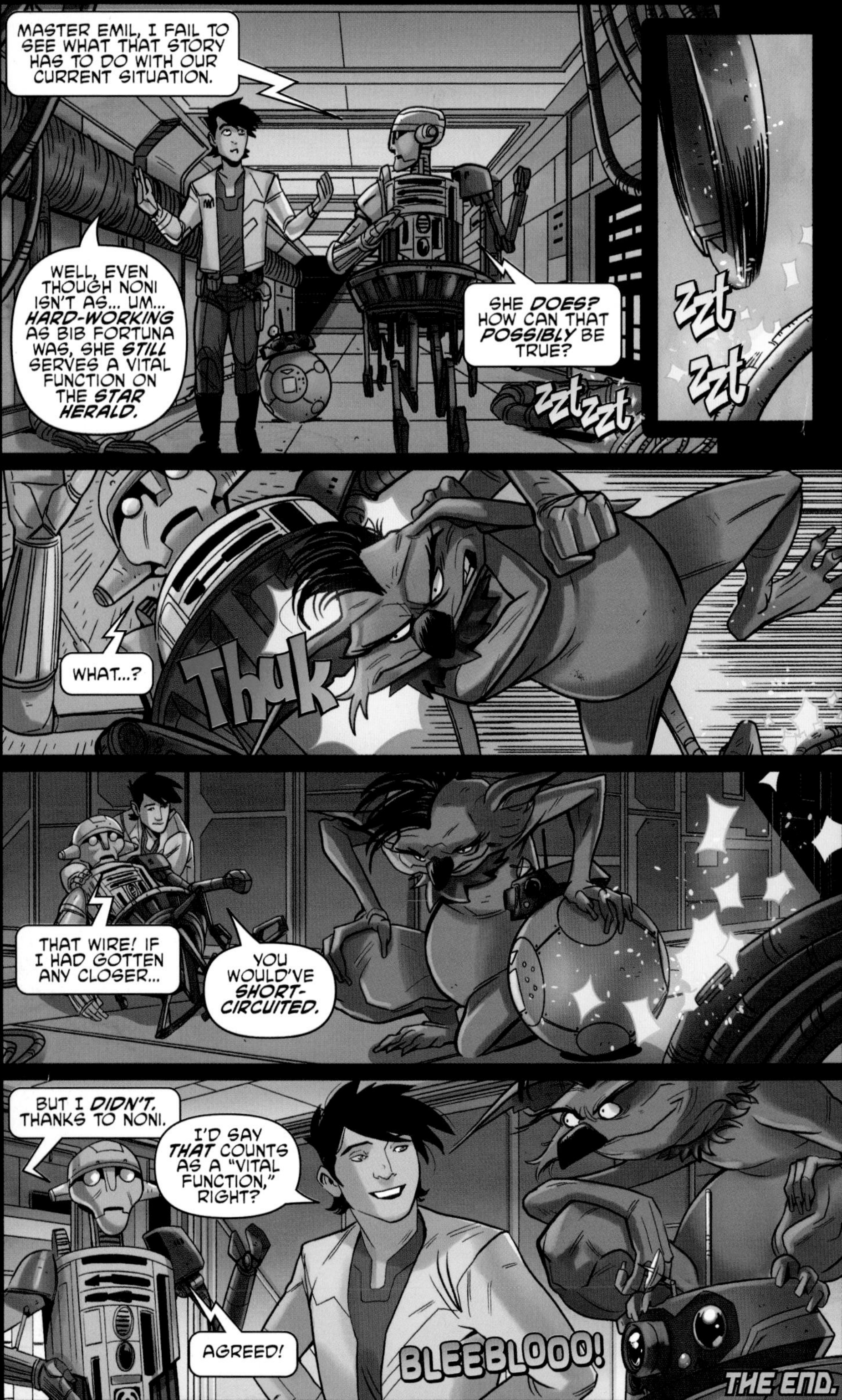
MASTER EMIL, I FAIL TO SEE WHAT THAT STORY HAS TO DO WITH OUR CURRENT SITUATION.
WELL, EVEN THOUGH NONI ISN'T AS... UM... HARD-WORKING AS BIB FORTUNA WAS, SHE STILL SERVES A VITAL FUNCTION ON THE STAR HERALD.
SHE DOES? HOW CAN THAT POSSIBLY BE TRUE?
ZZT ZZT
ZZT
ZZT
WHAT...?
THUK
THAT WIRE! IF I HAD GOTTEN ANY CLOSER...
YOU WOULD'VE SHORT-CIRCUITED.
BUT I DIDN'T. THANKS TO NONI.
I'D SAY THAT COUNTS AS A "VITAL FUNCTION," RIGHT?
AGREED!
BLEEBLOOO!
THE END.

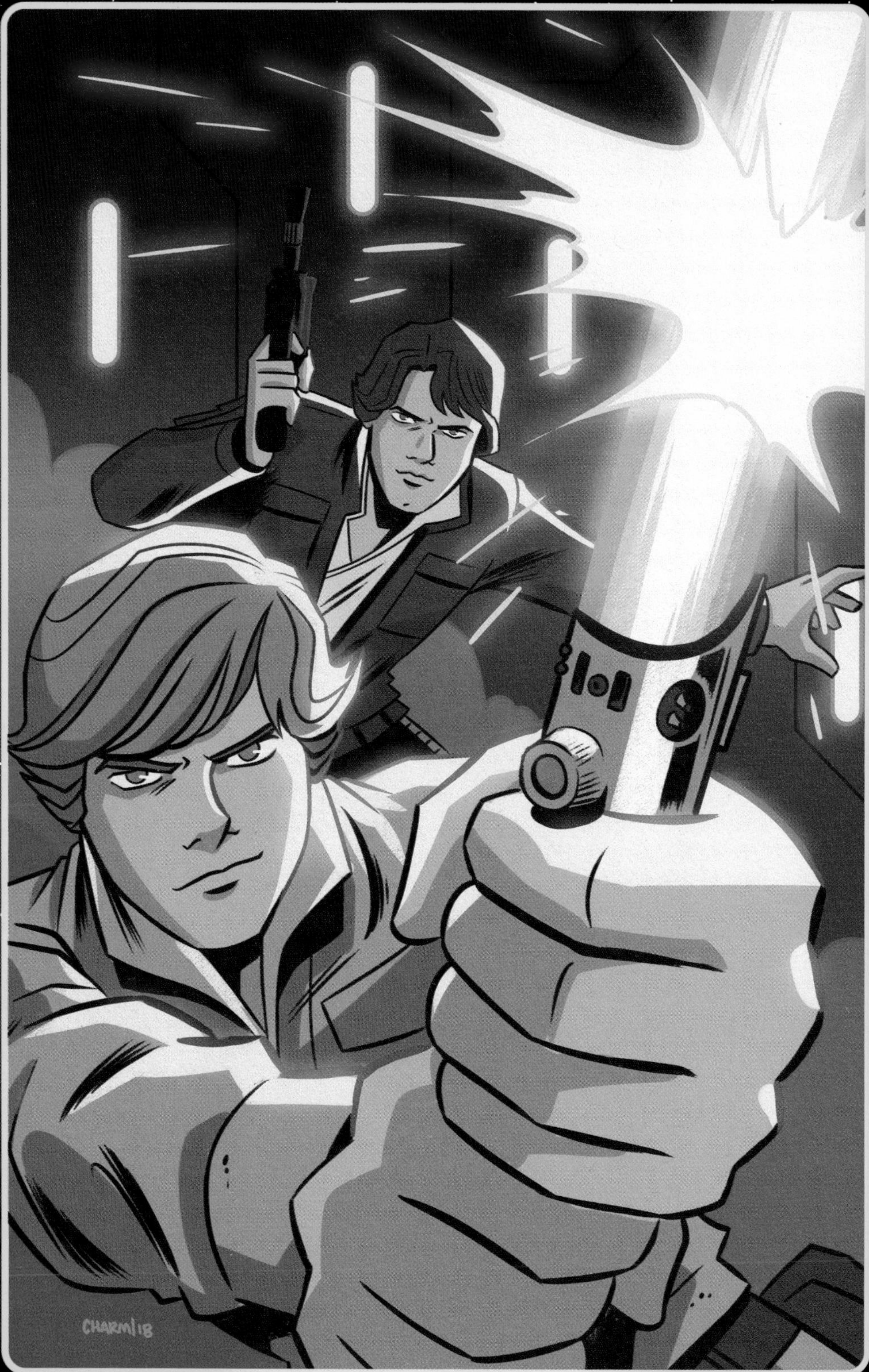
CHARM|18

Art by Derek Charm

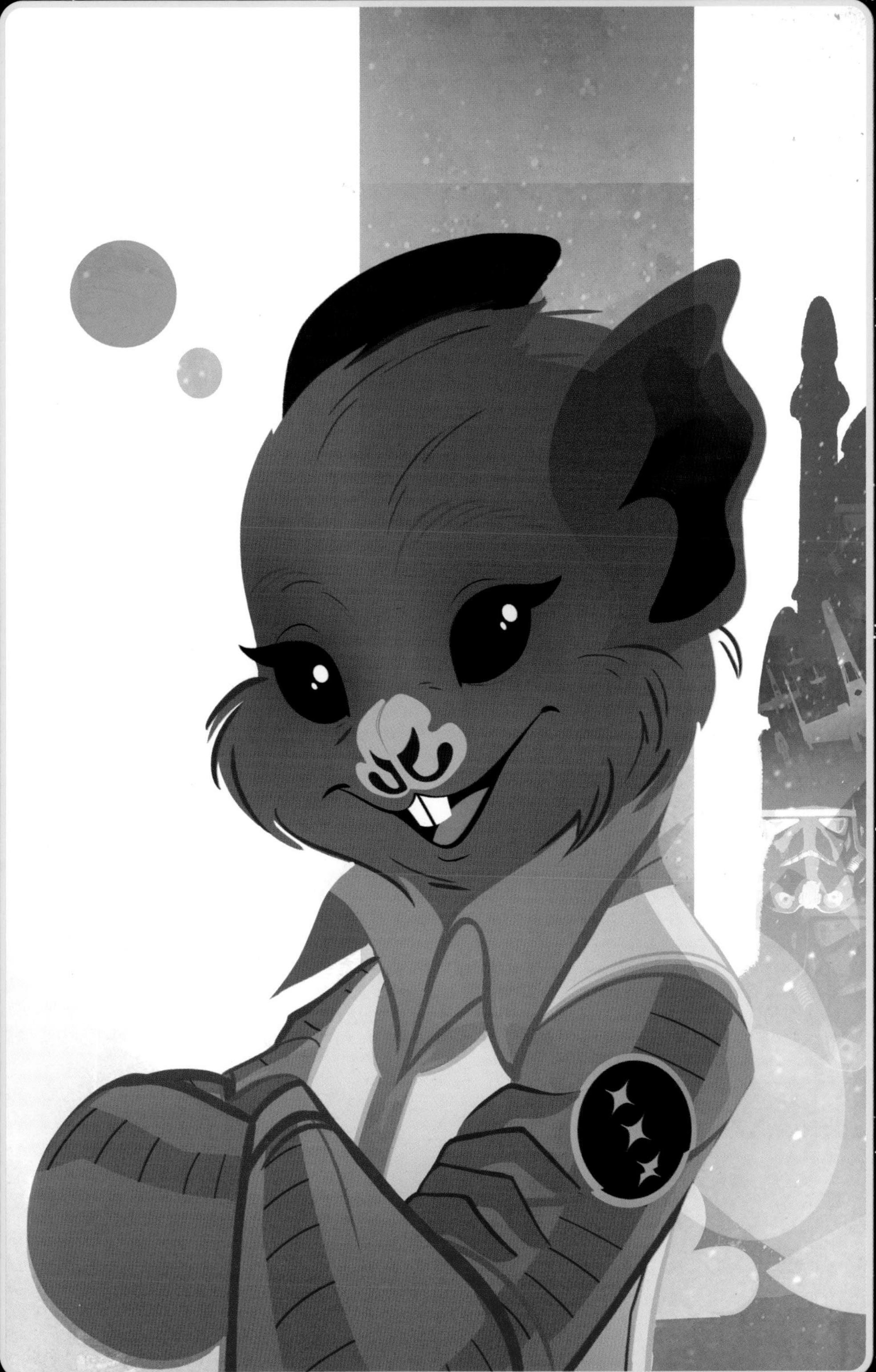

Art by Nicoletta Baldari

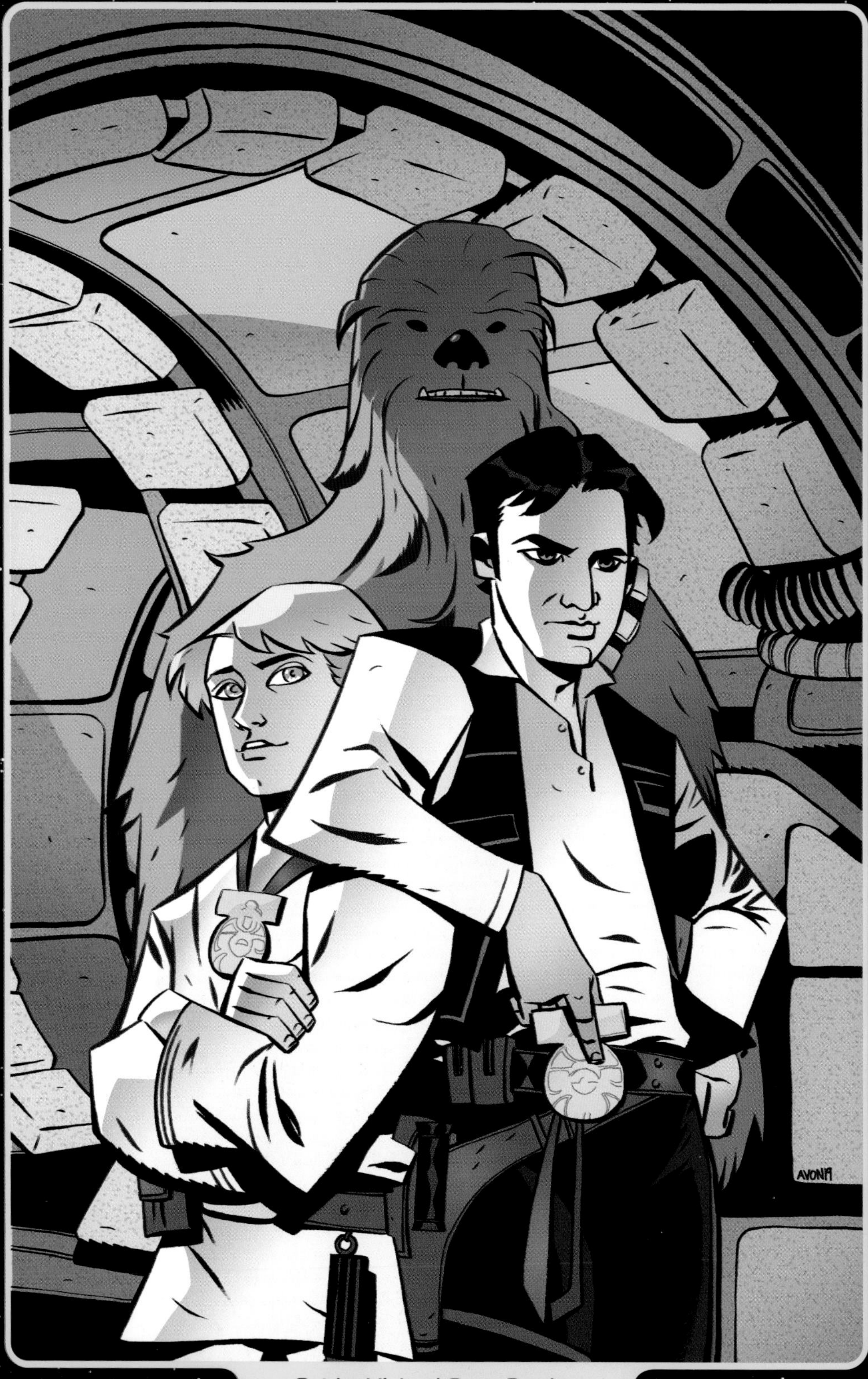
AVON19

Art by Michael Avon Oeming

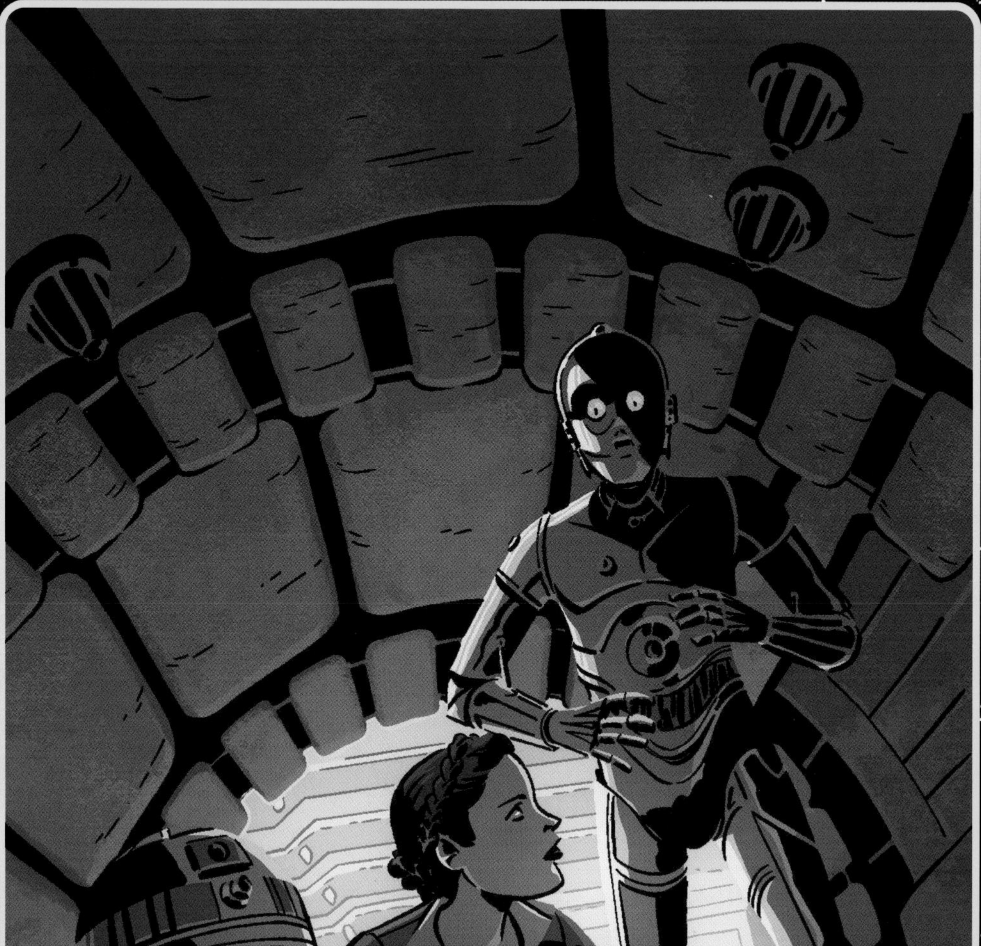

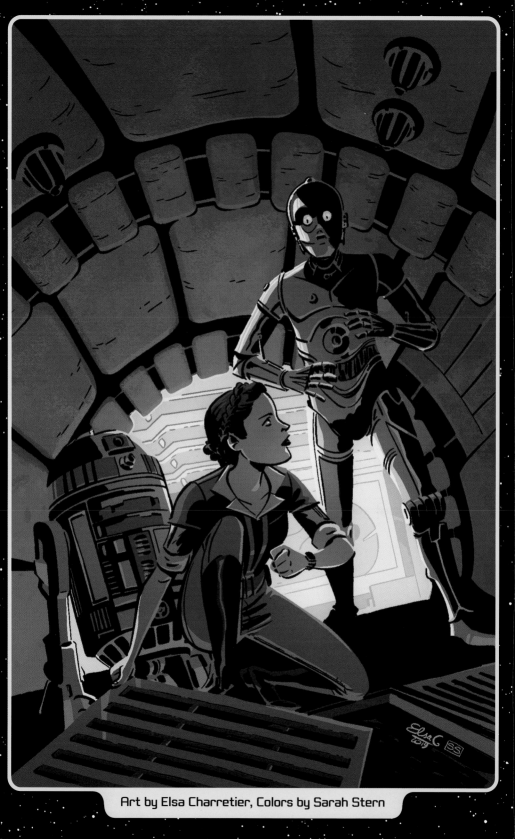

Art by Elsa Charretier, Colors by Sarah Stern

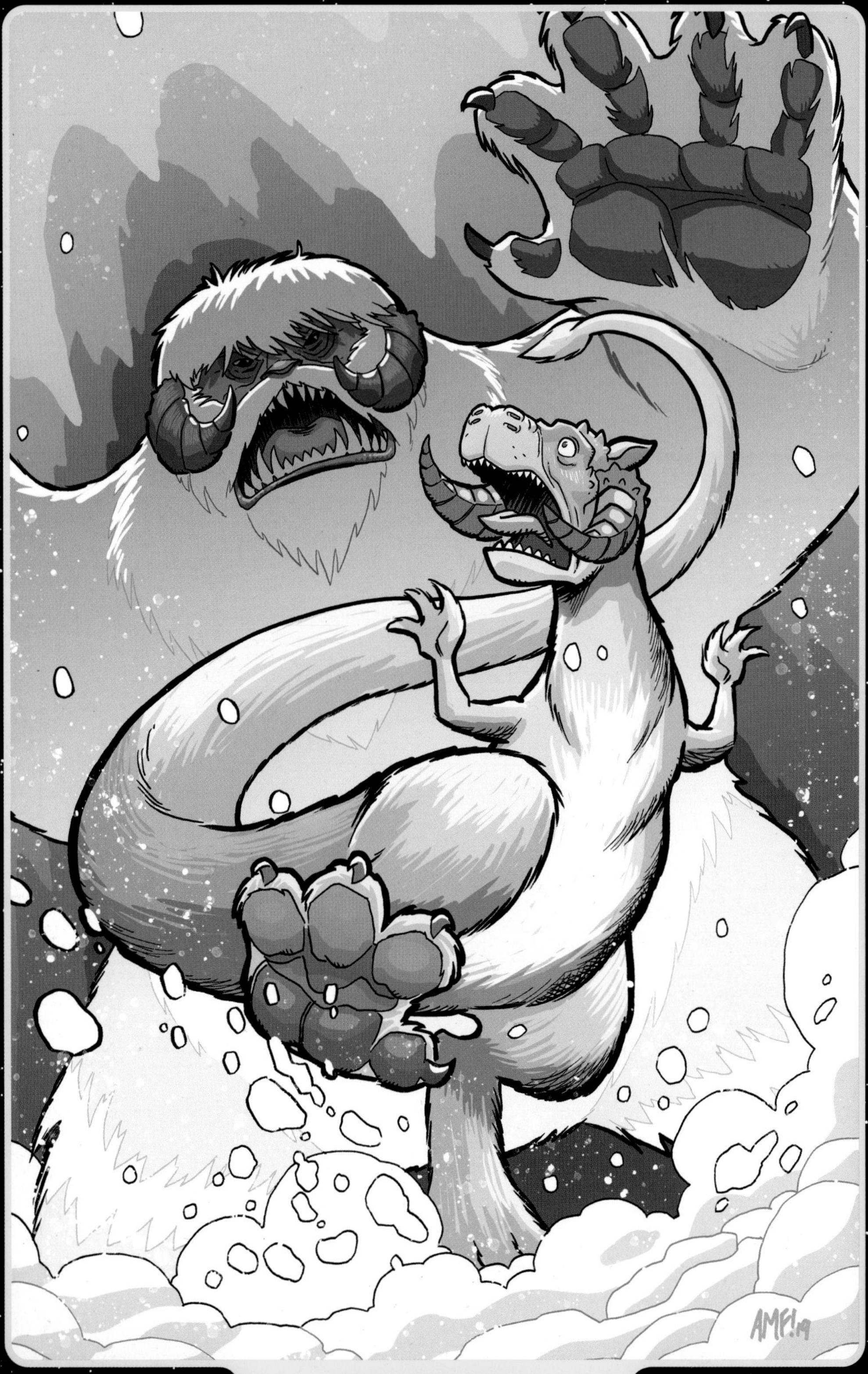

Art by Tony Fleecs

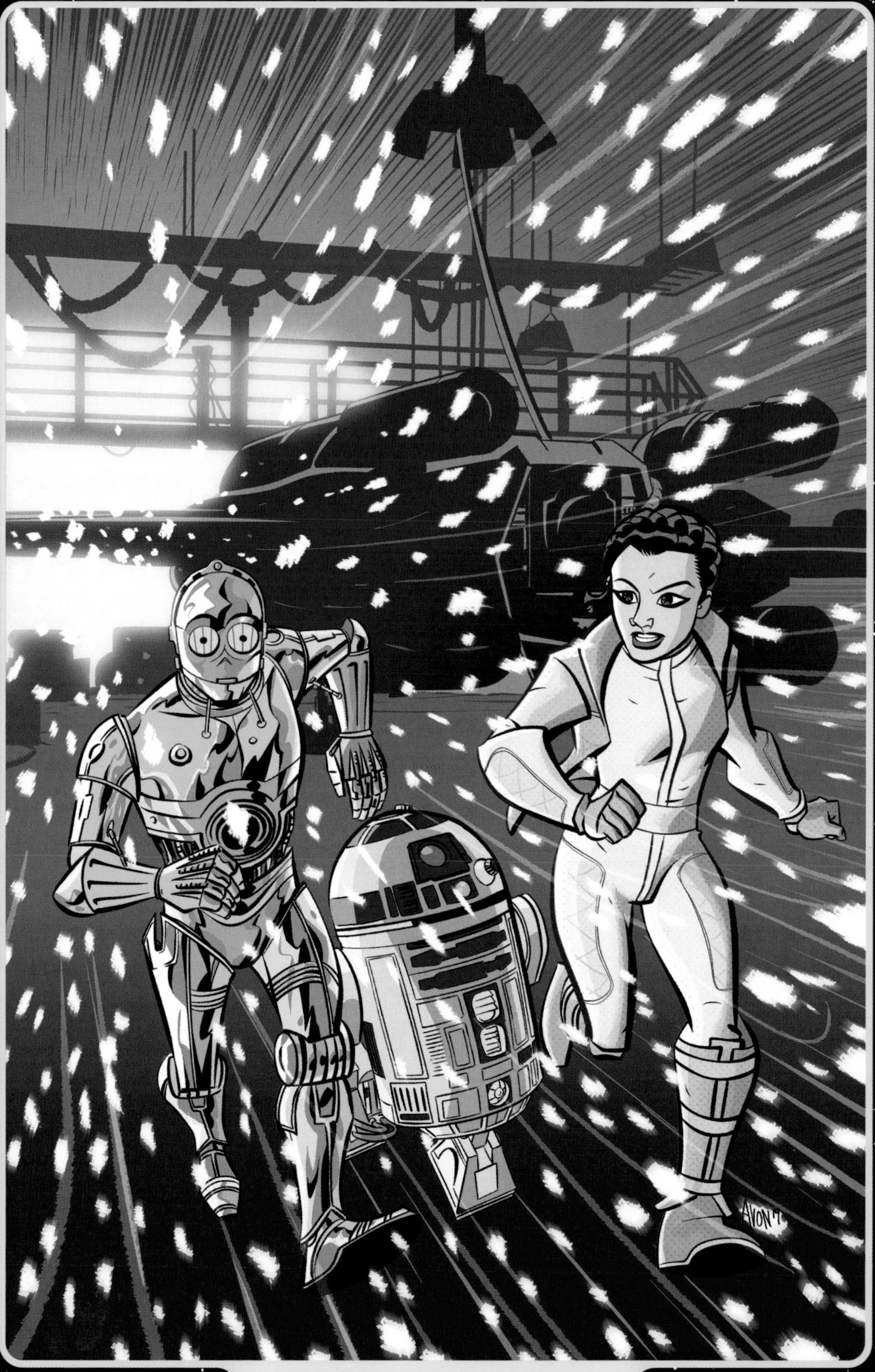
AVON '19

Art by Michael Avon Oeming

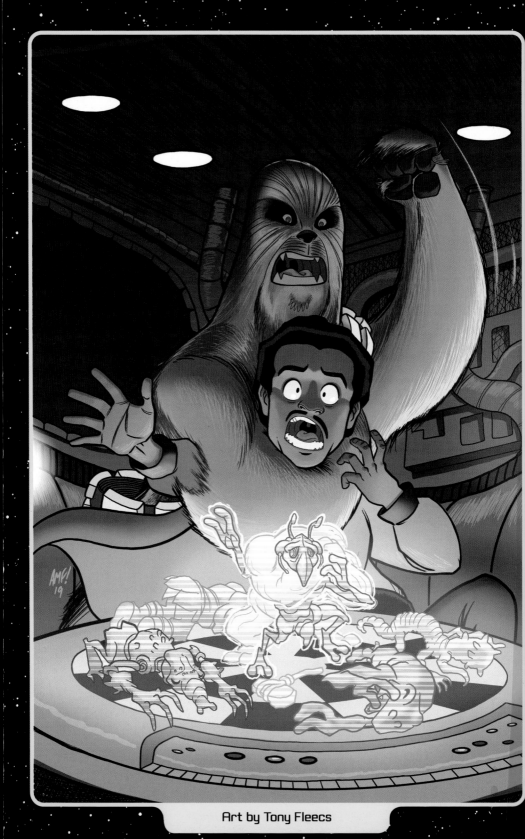

Art by Tony Fleecs

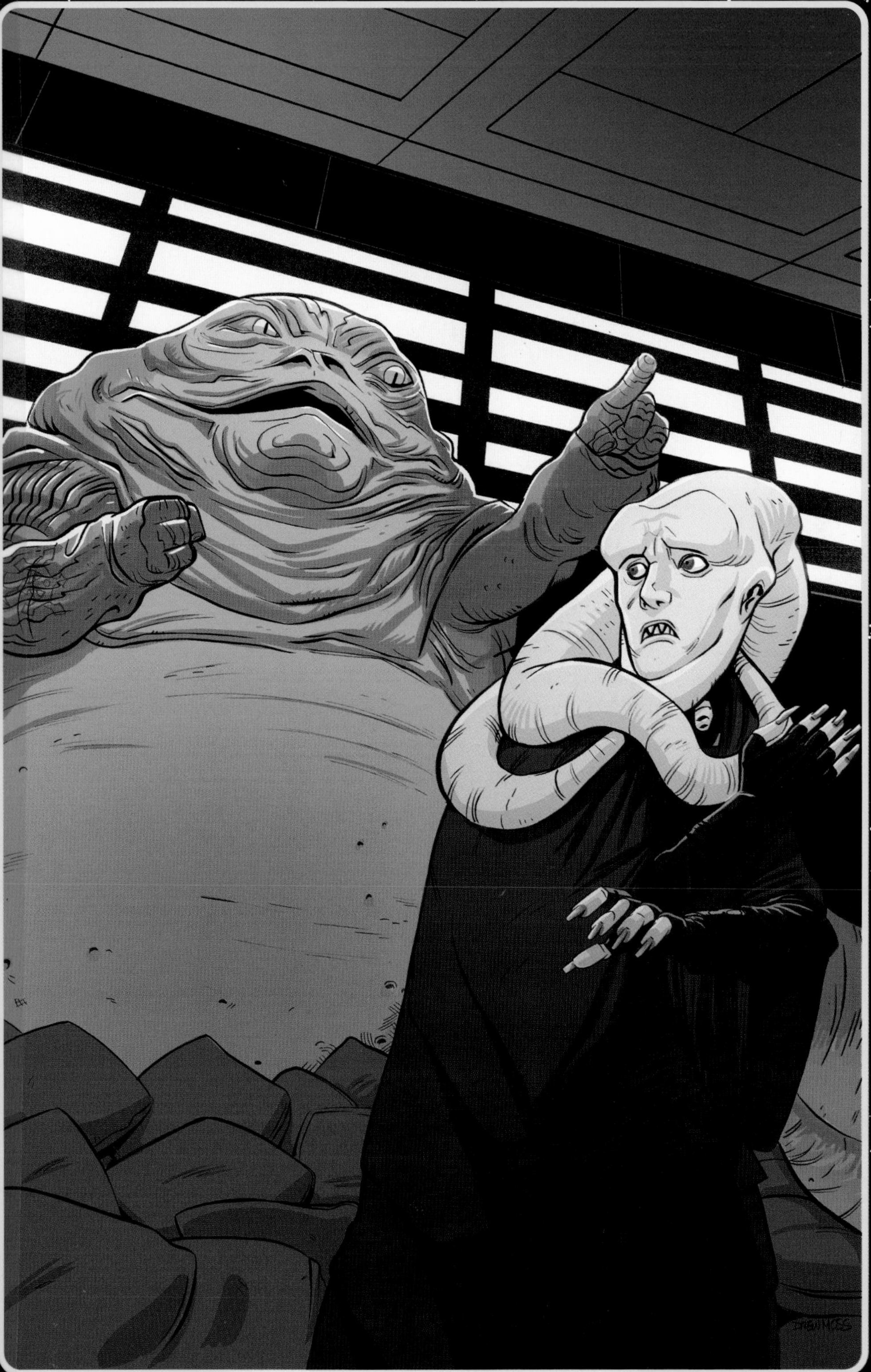
DREW MOSS

Art by Drew Moss

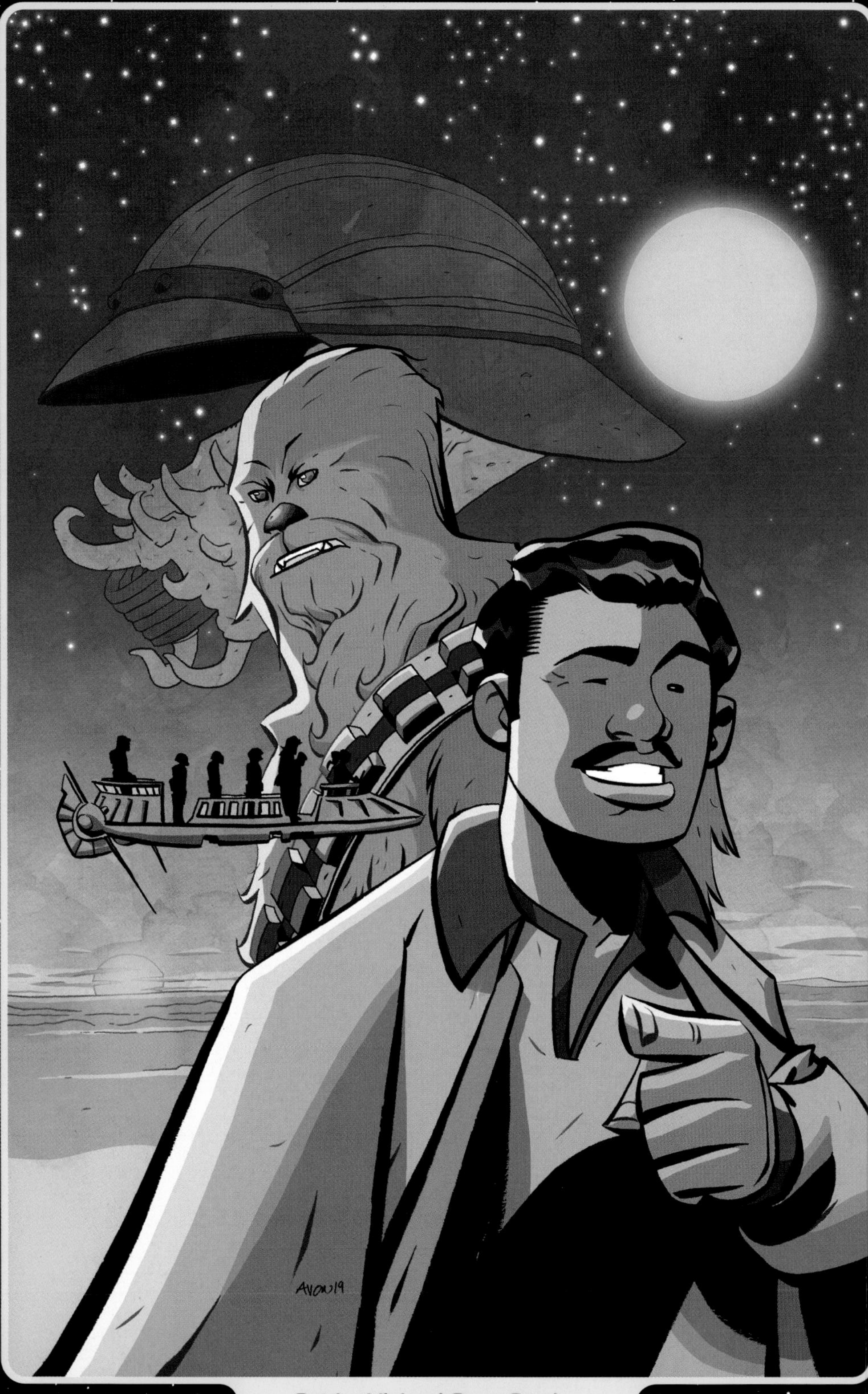
AVON19

Art by Michael Avon Oeming

WUHER

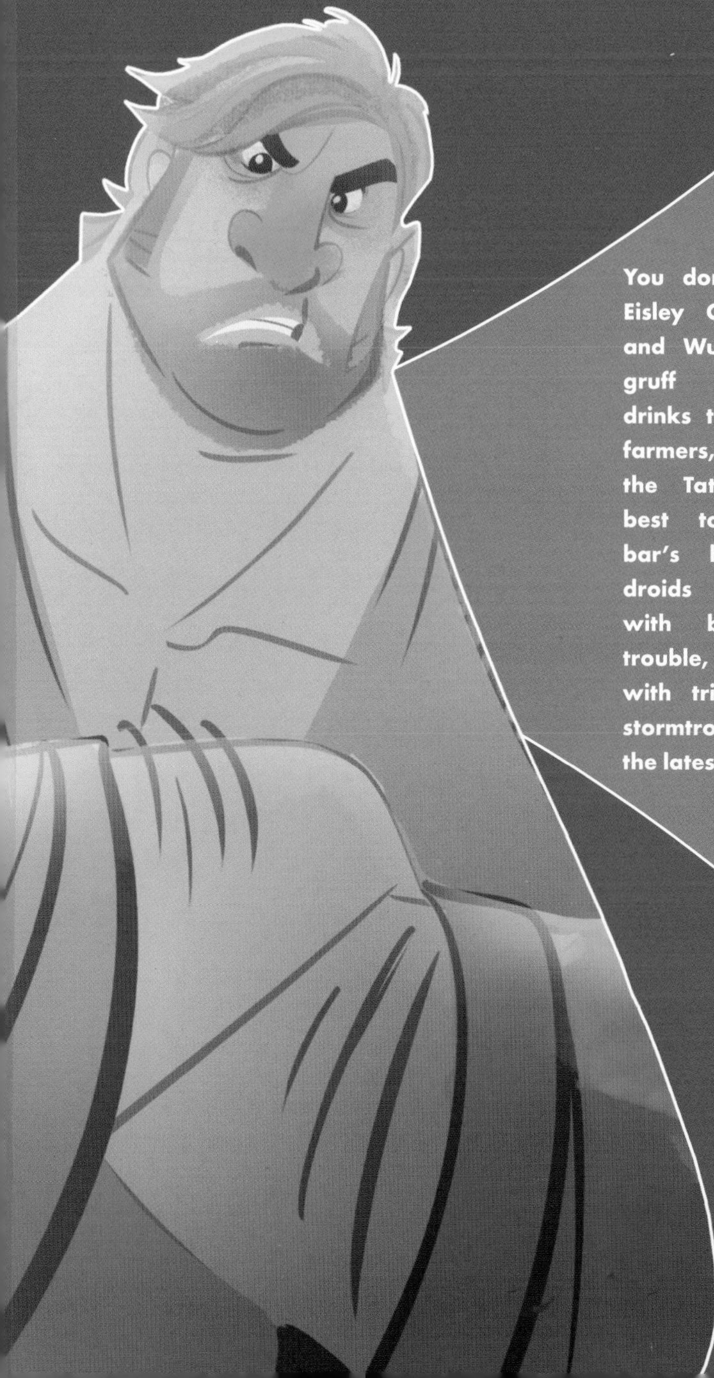

You don't survive in the Mos Eisley Cantina by being nice, and Wuher is a survivor. The gruff bartender dispenses drinks to the spacers, moisture farmers, and barflies escaping the Tatooine heat; does his best to enforce the seedy bar's handful of rules (no droids and no settling fights with blasters); and avoids trouble, whether it begins with trigger-happy patrons or stormtroopers investigating the latest incident.

ALEENA

Aleena are a short, blue- and scaly-skinned people, featuring large mouths filled with tiny teeth. They are a friendly people, welcoming the clone army and seeking peace with fellow co-habitors of Aleen. The podracer Ratts Tyerell is an Aleena.

SHRIV

A grouch with a heart of gold, Shriv commands Danger Squadron in the Rebel Alliance. Shriv—a longtime friend of Lando Calrissian and ally of Leia Organa—is a reliable officer in the rebellion's ranks, having assisted in the Liberation of Sullust, Battle of Endor, and other key victories.

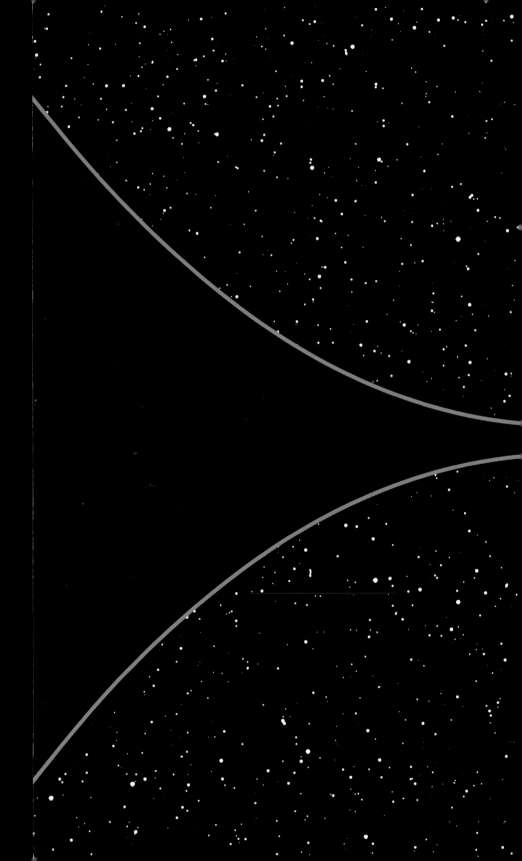